LOSING GRIP

Becky – Enjoy!

Angela K. Bennett

LOSING GRIP

A NOVEL

ANGELA K. BENNETT

TATE PUBLISHING
AND ENTERPRISES, LLC

Published by Tate Publishing & Enterprises, LLC
127 E. Trade Center Terrace | Mustang, Oklahoma 73064 USA
1.888.361.9473 | www.tatepublishing.com

Tate Publishing is committed to excellence in the publishing industry. The company reflects the philosophy established by the founders, based on Psalm 68:11,
"The Lord gave the word and great was the company of those who published it."

Published in the United States of America

ISBN: 978-1-61346-877-7
1. Fiction / Coming of Age
2. Social Science / Sexual Abuse & Harassment
11.11.07

Dedicated to Scott A. Grimsrud,
September 10, 1963–March 19, 2009.

PART ONE
JUNIOR HIGH

CHAPTER ONE

"Hey, get off the roof!" my mom shouted from somewhere below. We both froze. Mark mouthed *get down*, and for a couple of seconds we just stood quietly, hoping she really didn't see us. Then we couldn't hold it any longer and both burst out laughing.

"Come on, Sami!" he shouted as he stood up.

Before I could take a breath, he took off running across the top of the cabin and dropped out of sight. "Wait!" I yelled, running after him as usual. I stopped dead in my tracks as I got to the edge.

From below I heard my big brother half whisper half yell, "Don't be a chicken. Jump!"

Just as I leaped off the edge, I heard the front door slam, and I knew if she caught us, it was going to be chore city. Hitting the ground my legs buckled and bounced up once, then somersaulted over like in the movies, coming right back up to my feet. Before I even had my balance, Mark grabbed my arm and took off running down the path through the trees that led to my grandparent's cabin.

Coming out of the woods, we ran smack-dab into our cousin, Monte, and all laughter stopped. He was a big seventeen-year-old creep who had been living with my grandparents for as long as I could remember. Even though Mark was two years younger and resembled a toothpick next to Monte's football player frame, my brother protectively tucked me in close behind him and stood toe to toe with that monster.

"Get out of the way, Monte." Mark growled through clenched teeth.

"Make me, little cuz." Monte said stepping closer. Trying to peek around Mark, he grinned. "Hey, Sami, you look cute in your bikini. Haven't seen that much of you this summer," He winked at me, and I wanted to punch him right where it hurts.

Mark knew exactly what Monte meant and was enraged. "Don't talk to her. Don't even look her direction, or I'll kill you."

I gave Mark a slight nudge from the back. "Come on, let's get out of here. He's not worth it."

Thank goodness I heard Mom calling from the other side of the trees. Mark grabbed my arm, and we took off back the way we came. I made the mistake of looking back, and Monte was staring right at me. "He's so scary," I said to my big brother. "Thanks for blocking me from him."

Mark stopped dead in his tracks and looked me right in the eye. "Sam, you never have to worry about him ever hurting you again as long as I'm alive. That scumbag will never touch you again." Then he turned, and we were back on the way back to the cabin as if nothing had happened. "Race ya!" he yelled, and took off running.

"Cheater!" I yelled. Letting out a laugh, I bolted after him.

When we came out the other side of the trees, Mom was shaking the kitchen rug off the side of the deck. She looked at us and yelled, "Come on you two, we have to get this place cleaned up so we can get back to town! In case you've forgotten, tomorrow is the first day of school. Bedtime tonight." I couldn't believe she was smiling the whole time she was talking. Mark looked at me and rolled his eyes. We both laughed under our breath and trudged up to get our orders.

Mom laid her rug down and picked up another one. As she shook, she ordered, "Mark, you get all the fishing and lawn gear put away. Sami, you go strip all the beds and put laundry in the car. I'll try and catch the cat and drug her so she's ready for the ride."

"I can get her, Mom. She's on the roof," I offered.

Trying not to smile she answered, "Right, and how would you happen to know that? I think you two have spent enough time on the roof for one day." She turned to give the rug one more quick snap. "Sami, run in and open a can of tuna for me, would you please? I think if I set it on the railing for a little while, she'll come down."

Being the obedient thirteen-year-old that I am, I marched myself into the cabin, got the tuna, and did exactly what I was told.

With all three of us working quickly, we had the cabin ready and the car packed in no time. Mom was taking one last inventory. "Hey, what did you two do with all those garter snakes you caught the other day?"

Mark looked at me, and I'm pretty sure my eyebrows where touching my hairline. "Ummmm," we both said at the same time.

Mom could see we were trying to decide if we should lie or fess up to something. She didn't even hesitate. "Okay, go take care of it." The two of us turned and headed for the boat landing at the far end of our lot.

As we aproached, a horrible stench wafted up from the shoreline. I plugged my nose. "Ew, that can't be what I think it is?"

Mark followed my lead and plugged his nose too. "Wanna make a bet?" We carefully stepped closer. As we approached the end of the boat launch and came to the beach, the vessel containing the ugliness was in our view. That yellow and white minnow bucket with the hinged lid never looked so ominous lying still and evil on the sand. Carefully, we approached as if it were going to explode. Suddenly and out of nowhere, I felt something warm on my back, and I was instantly lunging toward the vessel of filth. I flailed my arms to get my balance just in time to land on my hand and feet right smack-dab over the top of it. Instantly I rolled to the side and onto my feet. "Mark, you jerk!" I screamed, scrambling to my feet. He was laughing so hard he couldn't even talk. Punching him in the arm,

I ordered, "Just for that, you're digging all those dead snakes out of there by yourself."

"Not likely, Mouse." He panted through broken laughs.

Fog, clouds, damp cold…These are the days that scare me when walking the dreaded two miles home alone. As I headed down the old dirt road, I heard the eerily familiar sound of the rickety old wagon coming up behind me. More days than not, they would find me. I didn't understand why he and his women couldn't just leave me alone. As the sound of the rusty, broken-down wheels approached, my pace and heart quickened with every approaching creak. Unable to control the panic, my body instinctively broke into a run, but my legs were numb and tingly from fear and wouldn't let me accelerate. Why is it that every time I needed to escape from this monster, my blood turned to stone and made my legs feel like they weighed a million pounds? No matter how hard I tried, my steps continued forward in labored slow motion. Unconsciously, I desperately tried to coax my body to cooperate, but it didn't respond before I heard the old man shout his orders in that gruff, evil voice I'd come to know so well.

"Get her!" he shouted from aloft his perch in the driver's seat.

"Why do they want me?" I asked through labored, gasping breaths.

The servant women exploded from the wagon, not letting their long, gray dresses hinder them at all. As I look over my left shoulder, I caught a glimpse of something swinging from around one of the witch's necks. *It must be something they'll use to bind me.* To my surprise, it's her Amish-looking white bonnet, like the ones worn in the days of the Quakers, swinging precariously as she comes ever closer behind me. In my mind, I secretly pray for the hat's strings to tangle around her neck and choke the life out of her.

My leaden arms continued to pump ever harder, even though I knew they're gaining on me. Quickly I scanned the area around me and decided to attempt my escape across a field where emerging from the soggy earth was an old barn that looked as if a slight breeze could topple it to bits. Interrupting my thoughts with his heavy footsteps, the man in black closed the gap between us significantly. They were so close I could hear their heavy panting. My blood ran cold as the anticipation of my imminent capture caused my heart to feel as if it was about to explode. Not a fraction of a second later, my head snapped painfully back as one of the women grabbed my ponytail and yanked it hard enough to throw me to the muddy ground. In seconds, the rest of the women held my body fast to the earth by my arms, legs, and throat.

Shouting at the top of his lungs, the master commanded, "Hurry up you hags, get her in the wagon before anyone comes."

Acting with total and undying obedience, the woman that caught me first took hold of my ponytail again as another blindfolded me. The wicked pair began dragging me toward the wagon. The weight of my body pulled hard against my hair as I was drug over the gravely surface of the road. I could feel a constant flow of sharp pebbles and rocks streaming over the waistband of my blue jeans into my underwear and down my legs.

After what seemed like an eternity, the screaming pain in my scalp came to an abrupt end. I knew we had to be somewhere behind the wagon. Just as the agony ended and my head started to clear, someone grabbed my feet, lifted me into air, and began swinging me back and forth. *What are they doing to me?* I thought just as I felt something slam into my back. *Oh my God.* Someone or something rammed into me hard enough to launch my limp figure into the air and onto the cold, hard floor of the wagon bed. Before I came to a stop, a sharp pain spiked through my head, and the world around me went black.

I don't know how long I was out, but when I opened my eyes just enough to see my surroundings, I discovered I was in the run-down, old barn that was to be my refuge, and someone had shackled me to a hook on the wall just high enough that only my toes swept against the ground.

Terrified, I shut my eyes as tightly as I could and prayed to wake up from this nightmare. Finally talking myself into that fact that it wasn't a dream, I opened my eyes to slits and froze as six women dressed exactly like my capturers marched in unison down a set of stairs at the far end of the barn.

Fear reached out and peeled my eyelids up enough to see more of my prison. Strange as it seemed, I was relieved to find that I wasn't alone. All along the two broadest walls of this decrepit old building, twelve other girls around my age were tied to hooks pounded into heavy studs just high enough to let their toes press slightly against the floor. All of us had been dressed in nothing but what looked like over-sized, white sheets with holes cut for our heads. Being the thirteenth girl had to mean something evil, but from somewhere in my brain came the thought of safety in numbers. It was comforting in an odd sort of way.

As I began to plan our escape, something strange caught my attention…all the girls' hair was shaved down to nothing but a shimmer of stubble. *Am I next? Are they going to shave my head too? Oh God, please, no, I prayed.* A shiver rattled through my body at the thought of what else the man and his witches had done to these girls and what was to come for me. Before the blood came back into my limbs, the witches had completed their descent down the staircase and had aligned themselves into an upside-down *V.* When their assembly was complete, they began chanting eerily, something in a language I'd never heard before and couldn't understand. Their evil mantra grew loud enough to rattle the windows around me as they approached. With each step of their slow, choreographed march, the foul smell of a mixture of human and animal urine, feces, and blood rose from the floor. It was like death itself was approaching. Feeling the wickedness in the room, we all bowed our heads, hoping not to be noticed.

Something inside me, morbid curiosity probably, drove me to lift my head slightly, cracking open my right eye to a single, tiny slit. I had to see. From my corner of the barn, I could see the old man as he turned and slowly made his way to the girl directly across from me. I could tell that he was carrying something at full arms' length straight out in front of him, but his body blocked my view. As the women hit a long, low hum in their chant, it was as if the thing came alive, for it started to franticly thrash in the hands of its captor.

Oh my God, what is it? I thought, trying desperately to see without being noticed. Slowly, I forced my eyes to focus on the flailing object dangling from the man's hands across the room as he turned to face the thirteen women in his coven. To my horror, I saw what looked like an animal, and the man had one hand on each side of its head. As I watched, he slowly began to twist his hands in opposite directions, and the creature let out a blood-curdling scream. I could feel my mouth begin to water. It was sheer panic that caused me to swallow the bitter bile that was beginning to fill my mouth. There was no doubt in my mind that if I let the vomit come, they would leave the screaming girl they stood in front of at the far end of the opposite wall for later and make me the recipient of whatever torture was planned for her.

I'm not sure if one of them noticed my heaving stomach or if a tiny sound escaped my swollen lips, but one of the witches at the back of the pack turned her head toward me and gave me a look that could have frozen fire. Instantly, I pretended to be sleeping and let my body go limp, causing the shackles to dig painfully into my wrists and hands. I tried desperately to block out the girl's screams, but I couldn't, and terror made tears begin to fill my eyes. *Don't cry, don't cry, don't cry.* I told myself.

Suddenly, I felt something touch my cheek. *What if it's a spider? A beetle bug? What if it's one of the witches or the man? Oh, God, please help me!* The thought of something touching my face made my stomach turn again. Even though I held perfectly still, the thing kept tickling my skin as it worked its way down my face. *Yuck,* it's going into my mouth! I couldn't stand it one more second. My eyes shot open, and my breath caught in my throat only to discover it was not any sort of creature or evil thing on my face; it was my mom tickling my cheek with her silky fingernails, waking me up to get ready for school. Man, I hated that nightmare.

As I sat up, attempting to rub the sleep out of my eyes, I discovered I wasn't in my bed. Once again, I had made my way onto my parents' floor.

From across the room, I heard my mom gently say, "Let's go, little lady. Time to get ready for your first day of seventh grade."

Embarrassed and half awake, I yawned. "Who you calling little?"

She giggled from behind the blanket she'd just swooshed up in an attempt to make the perfect bed. "You. Now go get beautiful."

Rolling my eyes, I flipped over to my knees and scooped up my blanket. As I stood, I made a pact with myself that now that I was going into the seventh grade, I would suck it up and sleep in my own room. For the past thirteen years, more nights than not, I have slept on my parents' floor. Time to grow up.

CHAPTER TWO

Growing up in the same school with the same kids forever can be more than a total drag. I mean, come on, once you're an outcast, you're always an outcast. The secret to survival in this place is to never ever let anyone discover any kind of weakness, no matter how big or small; for some of the mean kids, it's better than finding a pot of gold. Unfortunately, I didn't have to even produce a rainbow or know any leprechauns for them to make millions off me. To be honest, kindergarten and first grade were actually kind of fun, but second grade was a different ball game all together. I remember the day it started. Every time the recess bell rang, all the kids tore out of the school as if it were on fire. It was a known fact that if you didn't get out of there in Olympic record time, all the swings would be gone in an instant.

Luckily, I was a sneaky, fast little devil, meaning I got a swing more often than not. Once I got there, I'd save one for my best friend Danielle Ivan. Her classroom was four doors farther down the hall from the playground exit than mine, and because she's kind of a chubby-chub, she pretty much couldn't keep up with a snail. So if we wanted to play together during recess, I had to be extra-super speedy to get swings at all, let alone ones next to each other. This became our ritual. However, it was never more important than on this one particular, slightly warm, late fall day. We, for the first time ever in my two years in school, actually had a new kid. This meant that I had to get swings together so we could fly high enough to get a glimpse of her or him. It was the most exciting day of our lives.

Knowing exactly what time first recess was, I watched the clock in Ms. Brenner's room with the death stare. As soon as I saw the little hand hit the ten and the big hand slowly approached the three, all that was left was to get the secondhand to the twelve. Fifty-five, fifty-six, fifty-seven, fifty-eight, fifty-nine ...*go!* I was up and racing for the door before the piercing bell faded away behind me. Racing out of the school, beating every other kid to the huge metal swing set, I triumphantly jumped into the rubbery seat, instantly pumping my legs all while holding onto the seat directly to my right. When Dani arrived, I drug my feet on the ground, throwing up rocks and creating a dust storm. Other than jumping out of the seat at the apex of its forward blast, it was the only other braking technique I knew. Before I came to a complete stop, she grabbed the mate to my swing and made a diving leap for it on her belly. "Hey, let's play twisties!" she shouted excitedly.

"Hang on, Dan. What's going on over there?" I asked as I pointed toward the colorful merry-go-round. Stretching my right hand up as high as I could stretch, I began pulling myself to a standing position. Once I arrived at a complete standing position, I pumped my legs as hard as I could, encouraging my swing higher and higher.

"It's probably a fight!" I shouted down to her as I reached the top of my back swing. "Hang on, I'll get higher and let you know." Pumping ever more aggressively, I tried to see who was going to get in trouble this time. Stupid me, I assumed there was a bunch of dumb boys fighting. At the apex of my forward arc, I discovered it wasn't a fight I saw; it was a mass of unfamiliar, soft, flowing, blonde curls streaming in what seemed like slow motion with the turn of the ride. Spinning freely through the air was a girl I'd never seen before.

"I see a new kid!" I shouted down to Danielle.

"Oh, that's Becky Miles. She's in my class, and she's from Texas. Cool, huh?" she yelled back, obviously rolling her eyes as if to say, "La-ti-da."

In my head, I silently prayed, *Please, God, let her be smaller than me…and a whole lot weirder.*

Just then, the bell to go in rang, and I jumped off my swing as if I was dismounting a trapeze in the circus, leaving Dani in my dust and concentrating on my main goal of getting up beside the new girl. That little voice in my head was in total control of my limbs…I had to see how big she was. However, some goals just aren't meant to happen. By the time I had wiggled and shoved my way through the pack of stampeding kids, the new girl was gone. My quest was going to have to wait until lunch recess.

The anticipation was killing me. I absolutely could not wait until lunch. The rest of the morning, my mind wandered at the prospect that my time as the school shrimp was about to come to an end. Even though I'd only held said title a couple of years, I'd love to shed it ASAP. It gets really old having everyone tell you how little you are all the time.

Finally, the sound of the noon bell snapped me back to reality, and I bolted for the line of hungry second graders already forming at the door. I thought maybe if I got out there fast enough, I'd get a chance to size her up a bit. Out in the hall, there was a huge crowd of kids gathered at the bottom of the stairs. There she was, right in the middle of the crowd…and she was taller than Alexis. Right then and there, it was as if I was a helium balloon and she was the pin. Totally bummed out, I dropped my head, blended back into the brick wall, and followed my classmates down the hall toward the lunch room, ditching off into the girls bathroom closest to the exit just as I did every day where I'd wait until the sound of playful voices hit my ears, meaning it was safe to go outside.

People don't normally just relocate to our tiny, little, middle-of-nowhere town, and since this was the first new kid our class had ever gotten, Becky was instantly everyone's new best friend. It didn't hurt that she moved all the way from Dallas, Texas, and had the funniest way of saying things either, even I thought her accent was actually pretty cool. It made her instantly the "Queen of Popularity," and she took her new royal status to the ultimate level. She drank up the attention as if it was an amazingly creamy chocolate milkshake with whipped cream and a cherry on top.

From the moment she walked in the door, everyone seemed to be under her spell. It reminded me of the master and witches from my nightmare. Only in this case, the master wasn't a man; it was a second grade girl with silky blonde pigtails and a Southern drawl. In fact, after only a couple of days in school, when she told someone to do something, they did it or got beat up by one of many of her faithful followers. It didn't take this Southern belle long to transform from yummy milkshake to spoiled milk. *Gag!* Outside of my nightmares, I'd never seen anyone so viciously controlling and able to manipulate people like she did. Unfortunately, she zeroed in on my idiosyncrasies right away, and the next eleven-plus years were pure hell.

Why did I always have to stick out in a crowd? I just wanted to blend in and be invisible. However, with her, any and every little thing about me was just another ring on the dartboard, and she'd lie through her teeth to get everyone to hate me, make fun, and start chucking darts. More days than not, I wished I didn't exist at all. Hey, if no one could see me, they couldn't follow her highness's orders and treat me like a total reject. What was so different about me anyway? Who cared that I don't know certain stuff? When I was in kindergarten, my new friend told me that when a girl gets married, she has to change her name to the boy's last name, and I didn't know. Big deal! Who cares? So I had a fit and yelled out in front of the whole class that no way I was ever changing my name to a yucky old boy's name anyway. It didn't mean I was dumb.

And how about in first grade when the teacher stuck me in the corner because I read slower than all the other kids? That didn't mean they should laugh and make fun of me? So I was behind a bit. I wasn't dumb or totally retarded, as she liked to yell on the playground or at the most embarrassing moments in class. "Come on, quit stuttering, retard. Can't you read, or what?" Uhh, I wish she'd get hit by a truck, but...

Shocking me out of my reverie, my mom shouted, "Hurry up, Samantha!" from somewhere down the hall. "You don't want to be late for the first day of junior high school."

"Okay," I tried to grunt back at her through a toothbrush and a mouth full of suds. Little did she know, my stomach felt like it was duct taped to the seat on the Superman rollercoaster. Just the thought of another year with Queen Becky and what blessed events she had in store for me made me want to hurl the breakfast I had yet to devour. Maybe this summer I would grow enough to catch up to at least someone in my class, and they would see that I wasn't so weird. Hey, I even got a bra. Good thing too. I was starting to look like a freak with these little, hard-as-a-rock marbles in my T-shirts and leotards. To tell you the truth, when my nipples, or should I say nipple, began to burn and a marble developed under it, I actually thought I had cancer. I called Dani right away, even if it was long distance. Two things I learned that summer were that boobs were sick, and why didn't someone tell me they would hurt so bad? What the heck is that? Oh well, AAA is probably a good size if you want to be in sports. Come on, have you ever seen those girls with the big ones try to do gymnastics or run? They look like they're going to need to see a dentist or a jaw surgeon. That reminds me...Sports, *yes,* finally! Maybe junior high won't be so bad after all.

CHAPTER THREE

If you've ever been to the end of the earth where only old people and relatives live, then you must have been in Middleton, Wisconsin—population: a whopping two thousand, give or take a couple of old blue hairs and a funeral. However, sometimes dynamite comes in small packages.

The decision to walk to school with the hopes of easing my nerves a little before school was an easy one. As I approached the front door of our three-storied, square, brick schoolhouse that educates a whopping total of four hundred kids from kindergarten to twelfth grade, I tried to give myself a little pep talk. How bad can it be? Getting older should be a good thing, right? Well, needless to say, that bubble was completely burst with the first person I saw when I entered. Standing in the hall right in front of my locker was a girl I knew all too well, Alexis Blane, with her beautiful blue eyes, long, perfectly amazing blonde hair all tied up in bright pink bow flowing from the crown of her head, professional make-up application, and what the heck—huge hooters. Wow, where did those come from? I know they weren't there last spring.

As you can imagine, all the boys were swooning around her and her posse of made-up, exquisitely perfect hair, cool-clothed girl-friends that used to be my friends too before Becky appeared on the scene five years ago. When did all this happen? Walking down the hallway, it was genuinely easy to see that some things are never going to change. I was still at armpit level, sporting un-kept, short brown hair blessed with abstract curls shooting out at random and stuck with the boyish shag cut I'd had since third grade (although getting longer I thankfully might add) and no make-up (Mom said not until eighth grade). Worst of all, I was hopelessly boobless by comparison, not only to the other seventh grade girls and the entire student body but to my cat as well. Oh, man, I had never wished so badly that I was "I Dream of Jeannie" and could just blink myself somewhere else. Maybe they wouldn't notice, and my lack of pubescent advancement would make it easy to sneak in, set up my locker, and get out of there while they were all admiring the popular girls and their new "toys." Heck, Becky wasn't there, so there was a chance that they might not be total jerks to me right away.

Too late, apparently I was as hideous as I felt, because just as I was silently wedging my arm in between two kids to open my locker, they all turned and actually said "hi" to me. Even though it was dripping with sarcasm, I told myself to think positive and tried to see it as an invitation of sorts. Forcing myself to ignore their snickering and eye rolling, I awkwardly joined in their conversation. " Um, anyone go anywhere cool this summer?

Turning to face me, Alexis said, "We spent most of it at the lake." She held her arm up next to one of the guys. "Gotta love my tan."

He playfully shoved her away. "Yeah, well, some of us have to work in the summer." They all laughed, and I felt a smile creep onto my face.

I reluctantly turned to open my locker. I desperately wanted to keep this casual conversation going. It was one of the first times Alexis was actually nice to me. Usually she was way too good to lower herself to acknowledge my presence. As I started spinning to find the numbers on my combination, Alexis leaned against the locker next to mine, smiling, and asked, "How 'bout you, Samantha? You look like you got some sun. Didn't see you at the beach, so where'd you get that tan?" She didn't wait for me to answer before adding, "Were you and that hot brother of yours at your cabin a lot?"

Hitting the final number on my combination, I pulled the lever, and my locker swung open. "Nice," she commented, "I had to have someone with muscles open my locker."

Inspecting my new locker and ignoring her comment about my brother, I said, "Yeah, we went to the lake every weekendand sometimes during the week."

"Cool." She grabbed my upper arm and squeezed. "Whoa, these aren't the bumps you were supposed to grow over the summer."

I pulled away. She flipped her hair, and I saw her wink at one of the boys. I knew she was making fun of me, but for some reason I didn't care. I liked the attention. Her comment embarrassed me and left me unable to respond. Inside I was glad she noticed I was stronger. Sucking up whatever I was feeling, I jacked my knee up to balance my book bag. Unzipping it and pulling out a new notebook, I finally got my tongue back. "Yeah, I spent most of the time at the lake in the row boat. I want to go out for the gymnastics team this year, and Coach Hephner told us last spring that good gymnasts are strong."

Just then the bell rang. I had to admit that I was a little disappointed at the sound. The attention from Alexis and the others was nice, whether it was genuine or not. When the sound died away, I looked around; still no Becky. Relief flooded though every cell of my body as we all walked to class together. It was gym. I loved gym! Maybe this was going to be a fun year after all.

As we entered the auditorium, a silence fell over the crowd of kids, and we all stopped dead in our tracks. Holding a bag of soccer balls directly under the basketball hoop nearest our entrance stood the most perfect specimen of an adult male to ever be created. It was at that moment that I realized "tall, dark, and handsome" was not just wishful thinking of red-blooded females but that one actually existed. I'd seen pictures of guys like this but only on posters of movie stars and professional athletes.

LOSING GRIP

The sound of a shrieking whistle broke the silence and then came a familiar screeching, "Get a move on, ladies and gentlemen! Take a seat on the bleacher to the left of Mr. Beaux! Hurry up, we don't have all day!" The voice was that of the gym teacher, Ms. Greta Hephner, who began her career teaching the T-rex how to chase and catch prey. Clad in her notorious, barn-red (and size), skin-tight sweatpants, brand new glow-in-the-dark white Nike tennis shoes with some kind of funky laces, lemon yellow Asics T-shirt big enough for the entire class to fit in at once, she never disappointed the fashion police. All five feet, two hundred pounds of her was perched on the second bleacher, whistle clenched between her teeth and a tuft of short, gray, curly hair bouncing to the beat of the music blaring from the gymnasium speakers.

She herded us all into the auditorium and motioned for some-one to turn the music down. The girls were all tripping over each other, as no one wanted to take their eyes off the hunk blessing us with his presence. Even my knees were weak just walking past Mr. Beautiful, I mean, Mr. Beaux, and a strange numbness took over all my senses. Girls were actually pushing and fighting just to get to sit in the front row. As if they'd have a chance. Whatever. I got pushed up to the third row with the boys, but I didn't care as long as my view wasn't interrupted. Plus, most of the boys were nice to me. Once we were all settled, Mr. Beaux began to speak. In a voice that could melt chocolate, he said, "Ladies and gentlemen, I am Mr. Beaux. I'm looking forward to working with you fellas this year in gym and possibly some you ladies if you're going out for track in the spring. Now that you are seventh graders, gym class is going to be a bit different than you've had in the past. Ms. Hephner and I will be dividing the class in half. Ladies, you'll be joining her, and boys, you'll be working with me."

I leaned over to my friend Jason Mahoney and whispered, "You think it's too late for a sex change?"

He laughed under his breath and jokingly whispered back, "Cut your hair. They'll never notice."

Ms. H continued shouting, "You will be required to wear certain attire for this class. All students must have tennis shoes, appropriate sport shorts, and a T-shirt with sleeves."

Before she could continue, Alexis raised her hand and whined, "Would that be what we think is appropriate or you, Ms. Hepher?" Her little disciples snickered noticing that she left the *n* out of Ms. Hephner's name intentionally.

"Are we starting that business on the first day, Ms. Blane? You know that your shorts must hang below your fingertips when your arms are held at your sides."

"I'll have my mom call you. Long shorts don't fit my body type. I have to wear the shorter ones in order to be able to move properly. You know how it is with us curvy women, don't you Ms. H?" Alexis winked, shook back her hair, and checked her manicure. Her little friends let out one of their nasty giggles in support and agreement.

Mr. Beaux interrupted, "I'm sure we can work something out." He redirected his attention to the upper portions of the group and said, "Boys, you are now at the age that you must wear protective undergarments at all times during class. If you'd like information on jock straps, I have some in my office. Please see me after class."

Then he looked at the lower half of the class and added, "...and girls must have sports bras." As the word bra came out of his mouth, I could feel my cheeks burn red. Unfortunately, my blushing was visible to everyone.

The worse part of all was that just as the words came out of his mouth, in walked Becky who, right on cue, added, "Mr. B, I have a question."

She continued toward the group stopping right next to this gorgeous hunk of gym teacher. Looking up into his amazing brown eyes, she continued, "I am of the belief that if people didn't have feet, they wouldn't wear shoes, so why would someone, say for example, like Sam (she pointed directly at me) up there need a bra?"

A dead silence held the room for what felt like forever, letting what she had just said soak completely in. Suddenly the crowd of people on the bleachers burst out in uncontrollable laughter. I felt myself melting into the bench I was sitting on and disappear into a fog of silver and then black. The next thing I knew, I was looking up at the ceiling, and the school nurse was stroking my forehead with a cool, wet rag and telling me to sit up slowly.

In the background I could hear Ms. Hephner saying, "Please bring a towel, soap, a washcloth, and any other toiletries you will need from home. You may keep them in your assigned locker. Showering and deodorant are not optional. Any questions before we get started?"

My heart skipped a beat, and I'm sure my face went white again as I realized I'd have to change and shower in front of these people. There was no way I was taking off my clothes in front of anyone. It was an extreme phobia of mine, and plus, it would give them ammunition to tease me with.

Just in time for the locker room tour, the nurse got me to my feet and left. The boys went with Mr. Beautiful to check out their locker room and get lockers, and the girls followed Ms. Hephner. No one ever gave me crap for passing out. I guess they had plenty of other areas to go for. Walking into the school's torture chamber for women, I could already hear her starting in on me from behind.

"Oooooh, look at little Sami all grown up. She's got a new bra. I didn't know they made 'em that small. Did your mommy get that for you at Toys R Us?"

Then laughter filled the step. I think I was more disappointed than surprised that this was her second shot at me, and she hadn't even been in school more than a few minutes. As we entered the door, my eyes shifted to the left where two blessed bathroom stalls with doors sat blissfully waiting for me. Yes, I could hide in there to change. However, how was I going to get around the showering part? As I was thinking about the shower situations, the sounds of chuckling arose from the other side of the room again.

"Can you imagine those gross tits in a leotard? I remember those marbles from fourth grade. I bet she doesn't even have her first hair yet."

With that one, the whole room laughed. Even the nice girls were grinning with the exception of one or two. Trying not to show how utterly embarrassed I was, I put my head down and told myself that when gymnastics starts, I'd show her. I'd kick her butt where it counts, and maybe when they see what I'd learned at club, I'd earn respect. They'd be sorry they ever laughed at me. I'd show them.

Unaware that anything was going on in the room, Ms. Hephner just kept on talking. *Wow, how can adults just shut out all of this crap? Are they all living in La-La Land, dumb, or just totally deaf? I hope I don't grow up to be that stupid.*

Coming out of my daydream, I heard her finally say, "Okay, now that you all know where to go, what to bring, and have a locker, let's head up to the gym and get lined up to go." Then she just had to add, "Samantha, you feeling better?"

I shook my head yes, and we headed back up the cement steps to the gym; all of a sudden, I felt my body flying forward and my legs unable to keep up. Skidding to my hands and knees, I could feel the eyes of my enemy staring into my back as she walked by and purposefully stuck her foot out to get in another shot. From her evil lips I heard her mutter in my direction, "Might want to be careful walking home, creep. I'll give you something that'll make you pass out forever." All I wanted to do was reach out and grab her foot, but I knew I'd be the one to get caught by the teacher and end up staying after school the first day. Not wanting to miss the first night of cross-country practice, I squelched my urge to retaliate by thinking about getting stronger and faster for gymnastics to keep myself safe.

Suddenly, I felt a hand on my arm and smiled as I saw one of my friends that I ran with offering to help me up. "Sam, you're bleeding," she said, pointing to my shin. "Don't worry about those girls. They just think they're hot stuff because they kiss boys and have big boobs. Little do they know, kissing boys leads to disease and motherhood, and big boobs are only attractive before kids. Then they're all saggy and gross."

"Mandy, you always know just what to say to lighten up a moment. Thanks."

"I just wish I'd been behind her when she pushed you. I'd have given her the shove of her life."

"You're funny. Don't get into trouble for me, but I really appreciate you wanting to stick up for me. What do you have next hour?"

"English, with Mrs. Dennison," she said. She mocked sticking her finger down her throat to gag herself. "How 'bout you?"

"Cool, me too. Wanna walk together?"

Flexing her arm muscles like a big body builder, Amanda chuckled. "Sure, I'll be your bodyguard, Mouse."

"Hey, who you calling Mouse?" I said, jumping up and down as we walked, trying to be taller than she was.

She gave me an accepting smile, and we both knew what the other was thinking. If there was anyone at school I could trust, it was Amanda Andreson. She was there for me last year when my best friend, Danielle Ivan, was diagnosed with cancer and had to move to be close to Children's Hospital in Minneapolis, Minnesota, where her doctors were.

Looking over at me, she asked, "How's she doing?" She could see the tears behind my smile but acted like she didn't notice, which made me like her even more than I already did.

"Okay. When I talked to her a couple of days ago, she told me that chemo sucked, and that her hair was falling out and looks like someone attacked her with a dull clipper. She said she and her mom had to vacuum her bed at least twice a night or she itched so bad she couldn't sleep."

Concerned and sad, Mandy stared at the floor. The two of us walked a few steps in silence. Finally, she spoke again, "That would really suck. I can't even imagine. Is the medicine working so at least it's worth all the nasty side effects?"

"I guess so, but the best part was when she told me about what she and her mom call 'chemo farts.' I laughed so hard when she told me about them that I literally fell off my bed."

"What the heck are 'chemo farts'?"

"D told me that when someone is on chemo, their burps and farts smell like a pile of rotting corpses crammed in a tiny porta-potty located in the middle of the Sahara Desert. The really sick part is that they have extreme hang time. They have to open windows and turn the fan on to get rid of the stink. It's disgusting. She said one time it stunk so bad, she and her mom both blew chunks. I guess the other night she had one so gross that they were afraid to turn on the light in her room for fear the methane gas would react to the spark of the light bulb and cause an explosion. That's when I fell off my bed." With that one, Amanda and I both burst out laughing.

"That is the grossest thing I've ever heard. *Nasty!*" she said, spitting out her words between inhales of laughter.

After a rather long laugh attack, Amanda and I settled down, and I added, "She said the doctors are pleased with her progress. Did you know they removed tumors from three different parts of her body?"

"No, from where?" she asked surprised.

"...behind her left ear, the back of her right knee, and in her left boob."

Shaking her head, Amanda said, "That would be so scary. Next time you talk to her, tell her to look on the bright side...at least she can beat every boy on the planet in a farting contest right now."

With that the laugh attack blew out of both of us again. We struggled to calm down as we approached our classroom.

"Seriously," Amanda said, "please tell her she's in my prayers when you talk to her next."

I smiled and nodded, and we walked together the rest of the way to room 201, Mrs. Dennison's stimulating English class. Actually, Mrs. D was pretty cool, but I would never admit that to anyone I ever came into contact with.

When we got to our room, Amanda went in first. Suddenly, she turned and gave me this totally devilish grin, came back to me, hooked her arm through mine, and walked me to a desk by her. It only took one look around the room for me to figure out that her smile had nothing to do with chemo farts and everything to do with what, or should I say who, was sitting toward the back of the room. Yep, it was none other than the bane of my existence that had tripped me only a few minutes ago. This mischievously crazy friend of mine led me right to the back, where she sat down right behind Becky for no other reason than to be a total pain in the butt. As she settled in to her desk and took out her notebook, she "accidentally" smacked Becky in the back of the head with its corner. Laughing under her breath and looking right at me, she winked and said, "Oops, sorry. I slipped." That was just her opening moment. For the next forty-two minutes, she tormented Becky at every opportunity. As funny as it was, I knew that I'd have to make sure my brother waited for me after practice so I didn't get my butt kicked on the way home. As luck would have it, I had to walk right by her house to get to mine.

CHAPTER FOUR

Unfortunately, first hour was the only class I had all morning with Amanda and the first of many with Becky. Finally, the lunch bell rang, and everyone headed for the door. To most kids in our school, this was the best social time of the day. Me, I just wanted to escape away for a moment's peace from the "popular girls." This year was awesome. We got an entire hour to do whatever we wanted at lunchtime. Most kids went home for lunch, but I just skipped the whole social/eating scene all together. Going to the cafeteria wasn't anything I ever liked doing. I couldn't stand to watch people eat; it was disgusting. Some with their mouths open, just smacking away, some with it stuck between their teeth and smashed into their braces, and the noise...Oh, my God, I can't stand the noise of hearing people eat. It is totally sick and nasty. How can they eat in front of each other? Gross! It totally freaks me out; it always has. In fact, I can remember the day I started skipping lunch. It was the beginning of fifth grade right after the summer that convinced me I needed to be either so skinny that I was gross, or I needed to be so strong that I could fight off anything to make myself safe. That year I started sneaking into the bathroom on the way to the cafeteria only to come out after the first girl came in from lunch recess. Before that, I just sat at the table and pretended like I was eating all the while my stomach turning at the noises coming from all around me. In fifth grade, I started running everywhere I went, and one hundred sit-ups and pushups a day was just a "good start." This was when my obsession to be safe from everyone that wanted to hurt me, as well as the best, strongest gymnast I could possibly be, began. Yep, a lot of things changed for me that year. Except for one…I still wouldn't use the girls' bathroom at school and usually peed my pants on the three-mile run home.

Hey, now that I'm a seventh grader, the pressure is off. I can ditch the school grounds and walk around downtown all lunch hour; plus, I can use the bathroom in the secret locker room that Amanda showed me. Thank God for small favors and Amanda.

After bolting to our hidden bathroom, I left to walk the streets alone. As I trotted down the sidewalk, my mind wandered. I wondered if I was the only one who tried to figure out really weird stuff when sucked into a reverie. Oh well, I'm still not ever telling anyone what goes through my mind. They'd have me locked up in the loony bin for sure.

Today my mind was focusing on butts. I guess this popped into my head because one minute I was walking my usual mach-twelve-speed along the sidewalk when I rounded the corner of an old apartment building and ran head first into the back of a rather bulbous old woman. Being abnormally short for my age, as usual, I was at butt level. It got me thinking…*Why does every living thing have a butt? And why do human butts all look generally the same, no matter if they are a boy or a girl?* If you really think about it, butt cheeks are really useful. They keep our bones from killing when we sit. *Hey, I wonder if fat people feel like they're sitting on beanbags.* That would be cool. Being only sixty-five pounds, I know that a big butt has to be way more comfortable to sit on than a skinny, boney butt.

I wonder how much I'd have to eat to get fat. Yuck, block that thought. *He* obviously likes chubbies. Just look at all of 'em. I remember always getting told to eat more. No way, not in this lifetime. Pleasing him is not an option. I'm going to be boney, boney, boney with muscles coming out of my ears. That way if he or anyone else ever comes near me again…

"Knock it off…just drop it. It's over." I heard myself say out loud. Then once again talking to myself added, "I know I can kick his butt." A few steps later, I added to my own private, little conversation, "Enough of the butt thing for today, weirdo."

Chuckling to myself, another thought popped into my mind. Not only does every living thing have a butt, but it eats, poops, pees, sleeps, and mates. Eww…why would I think about mating? That's sick. But really, we aren't all that different, humans and animals. Weird, I know, but how am I supposed to control my mind? When dumb questions and conversations like this take place in my brain, it's not a mystery why people give me crap. Man, even I think I'm weird sometimes. What the heck? Where does this stuff come from?

Interrupting my own self-chastising, I looked at my watch and realized I only had about seven minutes until the bell rang for fifth hour. I took off running, as I had to get all the way back to school, to my locker, and to class in that small amount of time. Secretly, I loved the challenge. Racing was so much fun. Actually, I hated racing against other people; that made me nervous. But I loved racing against myself. Trying to beat myself seemed like a way better way to know if I was getting stronger or not.

Flying across the playground, I smiled, waved, and yelled to the little kids out playing for lunch recess. They were always really cool to me. Probably because I babysat most of them or our parents are friends. I actually liked being around the little kids. They are nice to me, and I'm taller than they are. Bonus! Okay, not all of them, but most of them.

Entering the school, I bolted up the stairs two at a time, only to run straight into my mom. *What the heck? She's never at this end of the building this time of day.* After she was done getting on my case me for running up the steps, she asked the question I'd been waiting for.

"Where have you been?" she asked, not as mad as I thought she'd be.

"Nowhere…just walking off my lunch uptown." I lied. Grownups never understand anything, so why try?

"What was for lunch?" she asked, knowing full well I had absolutely no idea what the cafeteria ladies were serving that day, nor had I brought anything from home.

"Ummm…hot dogs and French fries." I tried to bluff. "They always have that the first day of school."

"Funny, my kids came back from lunch and were raving about the awesome pizza the ladies made. They also thought the ice cream sandwiches were to die for. You didn't eat lunch again did you, Sam? Let's not go through that again this school year, please. You have to eat. Follow me, I have an apple in my room, and I'm going to watch you eat it."

"But, I'll be late for math, and I can't start the year like that, Mom." I hastily interrupted, wriggling my hand out of hers and starting to walk away.

"Okay, I'll put it in your locker during my break. Eat it before you go to practice or you're going to get sick. You're nothing but skin and bones now, and that's not good for you."

"Deal!" I yelled back to her from halfway down the hall toward my locker, with crossed fingers of course. "I promise I'll eat it right after school." I turned and quickly headed for my locker, half walking, half running.

CHAPTER FIVE

With the hot September sun beating in the windows, sitting in class the rest of the afternoon was torture. Why do they always put all the dumb classes after lunch when all you want to do is get outside and be free? One good thing happened; I only had one class with Becky—science, gag. She saw me and knew that since she was the only one of her little group in this class, she had all the boys to herself. Lucky for her she had on her short shorts today. That way her butt hung right out in the open for all to see, and the boys didn't miss a moment like that. Too bad she had albino-white skin, and let's just say we all could have done without the cottage cheese show. Becky wasn't fat, but she could stand to run a few miles. Actually, some of the boys even called her "Jell-O butt" and "thunder thighs." One of them even asked her if she got her boobs out of a pizza box this past summer. With that one, I couldn't hold it any longer and finally let the roaring laughter come flying out; so did everyone else in the room.

Sucking in her gut and arching so as to stretch out the skin on her butt and belly, she turned slyly around and looked straight at me, "What are you laughing at, you anorexic little creep?"

"You." I sneered back, brave now that none of her little clones was with her. "Every nasty inch of you. I thought you had one of your nasty friends with you until I realized it was just your butt." It was at that point one of the cutest guys in my class high-fived me. If there was ever a time to feel like I mattered and was accepted, that was it. I'd slammed her and got noticed by one of the most popular guys in our school.

"Here comes Reicker. Shh," warned one of the smart girls through her final chuckle. She even winked at me as she turned back around in her desk. I saw the rest of the girls that Becky and her crew are usually mean to smile and chuckle to themselves. Man this felt good. I never realized so many people thought she was as mean as I did. I guess everyone was just scared of her and her little puppets. *Maybe I'm not so alone in all of this.*

When the final bell of the day rang, I bolted to my locker and then to the locker room as fast as I could without getting busted. Even though there were only a few girls on our cross-country team, I had to get down there and be changed before anyone else got there.

Flying through the door, I ran smack into one of the seniors. *Crap!* "Hi," I said out loud while in my mind I was scrambling to think of how I was going to get out of this one. *Now what do I do? I can't change in front of her. She'll see. How the heck did she get here so fast? I do have my gym bag on my shoulder,* I thought. Okay, plan. Quickly, I said, "Uh oh, I forgot a book in my locker. I'll be back in a sec."

"Hurry, coach gets crabby if anyone is late."

"No prob!" I shouted back over my shoulder, totally planning on being dressed and ready to roll before I got back. *This sucks. I thought Mandy said no one would be down here except us. She must have meant just the runners and thought I just meant that I didn't want to change with girls' basketball players and cheerleaders, which is where Becky and the other girls would be. This sucks. Okay, I'll just hit the bathroom at the end of the gym that no one uses.*

On my way back up the stairs, I ran into Amanda. "Hey, Mouse, where are you going? This is the right spot."

"I know. I forgot my math book. Be right back."

"We don't have math homework. Come on."

Crap, busted. "Oh yeah, I forgot," I said, heading toward her, trying not to look guilty of lying.

Once we got through the door, I discovered that things were going to be just fine. Right around the corner was a sanctuary with my name on it. A separate bathroom made special just for me. Relief flooded me as I headed straight for that little stall around that blessed corner.

Seconds later, I emerged ready for action. "Let's roll!" I shouted at Amanda.

To which she replied, "Holy crap, how'd you do that so fast?"

"Lots of practice," I smiled, giving her a shove with my knee as she was attempting to tie her tennis shoe.

"Watch it, mousey girl, or I'll sic Becky and her gang on you," she said, laughing from her new seat on the floor. Giving her my hand, I yanked her off the floor.

"Hey, did you happen to check the sheet to see what we had to do tonight?" I asked.

"Yep, and you'll just have to follow me if you want to know what it is," she teased.

"I usually do, Speedy Gonzalez!" I shot back. She caught my compliment and said, "Go easy on yourself. You're usually right on my heels."

A few seconds later, she teasingly added in a low, muscleman voice, "Hey, now that I think about it, are you just using me for a draft? Girl, now I'm pissed. You'd better watch out. I'm totally telling Becky and her coven on you."

I couldn't help but laugh. "Oh yeah, you're tough," I spit out, leaning close to her face, flexing my skinny yet muscular biceps back at her. Amanda rolled her eyes and then suddenly grabbed me around the neck in a girlie-girl headlock, pulling me up the stairs and outside where the rest of the team was stretching. With a quick sweep of my leg to the front, we both went tumbling down. As we began to fall, one of the boys yelled, "Dog pile!" We were instantly buried under a mound of about four or five runners. Just then, Coach Simms came out of the door, saw what was going on, and decided to join in. Everyone let out a huge groan as she jumped onto the pile of kids. Good thing she's a little person or that could have really been ugly.

"Get off! Get off!" Mandy and I laughed, trying to squirm out from under the pile of people.

"Oops, we're supposed to be a cross-country team, not the wrestling team." Coach giggled, pushing herself up and grabbing the arm of another, helping her to her feet as well. "I can see this is going to be a fun season. I trust you all will have this much energy and zip out there on the open road. This afternoon, we're going to do what I like to call my 'push-till-you-puke' runs. It's four miles of pure torture. Yes! So, get stretched and head out. Check in with me when you get back. The first one to blow chunks gets a prize. I'll tell you what that is when you get back."

"Oh boy," Bridget, a junior, moaned, smiling at the coach and the rest of us, which caused a wave of sarcastic moans. Coach knew we were just kidding around. She knew that secretly all runners love torturing themselves. I mean, after all, it hurts like crap. I guess that's one reason I took it up. The other reason is that when I'm out there on the open road, no one bugs me, and I can just think my goofy thoughts.

Jogging along by myself, I noticed a tattered, old, dirty teddy bear lying in the ditch. I wondered if it was lost or thrown out on purpose. *Was it loved or one of those toys that was constantly being mistreated by one of those yucky kids? I bet that little guy would be happy if I ran it through the washing machine and put it on my bed next to all my other buddies. I know a girl my age shouldn't still sleep with, I mean, have stuffed animals on her bed. Too bad. They make me feel safe in the night. When I'm surrounded by buddies, stuffed or not, I know I won't wake and find the Master standing over me, hurting me.*

"I hate that rat bastard, and I hope his peter fell off from that old, rusty fishhook I slammed in him," I uttered out loud to myself.

Shocked by the sound of my own voice, I discovered I was really moving. Even Amanda was way behind me, or so I thought.

"Who's Peter, and when did you go fishing?" Amanda asked with a confused look on her face. *Where did she come from? I thought she was way back there.*

I couldn't help but smile mostly from relief as I realized she didn't hear exactly what I'd said. "Umm…" I stalled. "No one. I was singing…sorry." Changing the subject I said, "Hey, I didn't hear you behind me. Where did you come from?"

Calling me on my subject change, she teased, "Have you got a man on the side that you're not fessing up to?"

"It's nothing," I said, my smile fading and my mind wandering off to the creep that I was really thinking about.

Apparently it was pretty noticeable to Amanda that it wasn't all fun and games. "Talk to me. I can see that whatever you where thinking about must have been pretty serious. You never sweat, so those have to be tears running down your cheeks. Come on, let's have it? I know it can't be Becky. You said 'He,' and I thought I heard you say something about fishing or a fishhook. I didn't catch the rest. The wind hit my ears."

"It's no big deal, just singing…I mean, tossing some thoughts around," I lied, totally avoiding eye contact with her.

"How come I don't believe you? You are always so evasive. Now all of a sudden you totally dodge my question even when you're in your own little world. Something is going on with you. I hope you know you can always talk to me if you need to. Whatever you say to me stays with me." Reaching toward me with her right pinky extended, Mandy added, "Pinky-swear promise. You can trust me. I'd never tell anyone."

"Thanks, Amanda," I said, returning the gesture. As we locked little fingers, I added, "I really appreciate that, but I promise I'm fine. No biggie. Really, it's nothing I can't handle." Looking at her as I spoke, I could tell she knew I was full of crap.

As our arms fell back into motion and dropping it for now, she shouted, "Hey, race you back!" She took off like she was being chased by a mad bull.

"What? You cheater!" I yelled, took a huge breath, and kicked it into high gear. She always knew when I'd had enough prodding. But now it was time to kick her butt, and I was in the mood to at least give it my best shot.

"If I win, you spill your guts!" she yelled back.

"You won't win!" I shouted as I caught up to her. To myself I mumbled, "There's no way I can let you."

"What was that, Mouse?" she shouted as she looked back over her left shoulder at me.

Leaning into her opposite ear, I yelled, "Nothing!" and sprinted toward the school.

In my mind, failure was not an option. However, Coach always said that when racing, use your enemies to your advantage, so I let Mandy stay a couple of steps ahead of me in order to block some of the wind and preserve my own energy for the last mile. When we hit the edge of town, I took off and left her in my dust. She was faster than me, so I don't know if she was letting me win or if I was running as fast as it seemed.

A block from the school, she was right on my tail. I don't know where she came from, but she was right there now. When I looked over at her, all she did was smile and wink. What did that mean? I stayed with her until the last few feet, and then it was all over. I dove for the door and touched it a split second before she did. Huffing and puffing like a couple of old, out-of-shape, balding, tubby smokers, she threw her arm around my shoulder, slapping me high-five over our heads with the other saying, "I want to see you run like that at the next meet. Holy Hannah, what orifice did you pull that blast of energy out of? Man, either you worked you butt off at gymnastics last summer or you really must have a secret that you don't want to tell." As we dropped to the grass, she leaned right up in my face, squinted her eyes, and said with her best Inspector Clouseau accent, "Don't worry little woman, I'll get it out of you sooner or later. You'll see."

We were sitting on the grass, stretching and laughing, when my brother came out of the school. "How the heck did you two get back so fast?" he said as he came over to where we were. "The guys just rolled in."

"We were racing, and I actually gave Miss Amanda here a severe butt whooping." I grinned, giving Amanda the look.

"No way," my brother Mark said, reaching out to rub the top of my head, which, I might add, I hated. It made my hair stand straight up. Sitting on the ground next to me, close enough to knock me over, he added, "Amanda, did you let this skinny little runt beat you?"

"Nope, it was fair and square and a total bribe. She has a secret she won't tell me, and I told her that if she beats me back, she could keep it or else she had to spill it."

"Must be some secret…is it a boy?" my brother teased, giving me a rather sharp poke in the ribs.

"Get real, you dork." I said as I reached out and gave him a quick forehead slap. Returning to my stretching, I said into my knees, "Boys are nasty. Besides, I have enough on my plate just trying to keep you out of trouble. What would I do with another pain in the butt hanging around?" I finished my stretch and jumped up, trying to hide the stiffness my muscles felt after that three-mile sprint.

As he leaned forward to stretch his hamstring, I took a hop, placed both hands on his back, and cart wheeled over the top of him, shoving his upper body hard into his lower, giving that hammy a really good stretch. Instead of getting mad, he shot me a knowing smile. He is the only other person on the planet I've told my secret, and he has been a constant protector ever since. God, I love him. He tries to act tough when his friends are around, but I know in my heart that he would never ever let anything ever happen to me again. His friends have always been cool with me. After all, I've been their crash-test dummy for as long as I can remember. Whenever they built a fort or tied a rope to a tree for a swing, they always let me go in it or on it first. If it wouldn't hold me, it sure wouldn't hold them. Sometimes I was scared, but I sure wasn't letting any of them know it. Sissies can't hang with boys…literally. Why wouldn't they want me to come with? I earned, enjoyed, and was grateful for every black-and-blue mark and scab I ever got with them.

"Wait here!" I shouted to him as I flung open the door to the school and went inside. "I have to get my bag." With that, I scrambled down the stairs to the locker room.

In a couple of minutes, I erupted back out of the school door in a dead run, only to run right into Becky, knocking her on her butt. "Sorry," I said, not looking at my fuming enemy on the ground, but at my brother and Amanda, who were still patiently waiting for me where I'd left them.

"Watch where you're going you stupid, anorexic geek!" Becky shouted at me as she got back to her feet. "Better watch your back after that, flatso. You'll pay. You can count on that." She sneered, walking backward in her cocky gangsta strut as she went into the school.

Although the door was already closing behind her, and thank God Becky didn't hear him, Mark shouted, "Who you calling stupid, slut?"

Mandy burst out laughing, totally catching on to the fact that he had just taken a shot at me about my chest, or should I say, lack thereof.

Turning back to Mandy and Mark, I stumbled over to where they were sitting in the grass. "What's so funny?"

Mark laughed harder and grabbed for my leg. "Relax, Mouse. She's harmless."

I jumped away from his attack, and trying not to laugh loudly, whispered, "Dude, you're going to get me killed."

"She just called you flatso. Come on Sami, you have to admit, that's a pretty good one, even for her," Mandy said, falling backward and then curling up into a ball, laughing.

Trying to get the subject off my boobs and onto something I could actually defend, I stepped to straddle over the top of Mandy, leaned down and got in her smiling face and said in my best French accent mimicking her earlier version of the great inspector, "I don't care about the boobless comment, but where does she get off calling me anorexic? Anorexic? Ha, just look at him! Well, I bet if he were to stick out his tongue and turn sideways..." I quickly jumped from my position over Mandy to right in front of Mark, pointing at him with my index finger right up to his nose and finished, "he'd make the perfect imitation of a zipper"

Grabbing my finger and laughing he said, "Watch out, Mouse, or I'll let her beat you up."

Squaring up my shoulders, crouching down to get closer into his face, I asked "You pullin' my finger, boy?" As the words came out of my mouth, I gave a quick tug on his finger.

His grasp tightened, and he said, "Yeah, so, tough guy."

Still pulling with all my might, I said, "You know what happens when you pull my finger. Better run." He lifted his leg up over my arm, keeping a tight grip on my finger, stuck his butt in my face, and did what all brothers love to do. He let the biggest, grossest fart ever. "Huh, beat you to it." Then just as quickly as he'd grabbed my finger, he let it go, and I went flying backward to land on my butt on the ground at Mandy's feet.

"Eww!" Mandy and I both grimaced, slamming our hands up to plug our noses. "*Gross!*" we said in unison as he stood there, pretending to blow on his fingernails and then brush the dust off his shoulders. He had every right to be proud of that one. Just as he was about to sit on the two of us for an encore, a girl he liked came out of the school.

"Wow! That was impressive." Jessie Bradshaw said as she walked by, bumping my brother in the leg with her perfectly shaped hip. "That's some nasty stench you have there, boy. You should bottle it and sell it. You'd make a mint."

Apparently, he thought I should have warned him about Jessie's sudden appearance, because he gave me a look that could kill.

"Don't give me that look. You had that coming." Looking at Amanda I said, "…and I thought Danielle had wicked farts. Gross!" I hopped up off the grass and put a hand out to Mandy, giving her a tug big enough to pull her to her feet. Then grabbing my throat as if choking, I gagged out, "Let's get out of here before we suffocate and die."

Mandy choked out, "Hey, you only have one brother who does that crap to you. I have to put up with it with four of them, and my dad's no better." Laughing and still holding our noses, we both turned and started running toward the street away from my brother and his perfect little crush.

About twenty feet down the sidewalk, I looked back just in time to see Mark shut the door of Jessie's black Grand Prix and wave good-bye. Miss Perfect pulled away from the curb and headed toward the stop sign at the end of the street. When she was far enough away that he was sure she couldn't hear him, he shouted in our direction, "Hey, wait up, you dorks!" He blasted toward us on a dead run. Two seconds later, he was right between us huffing and puffing, "I've got a fresh one for ya! He wrapped his arms around our shoulders, pulling us both into headlocks and said, "It just wouldn't be fair for me to not share everything I have with my little sissy and her bestest bud. And now that I've got you in my trap, you're both doomed." With that, Mark let out his best evil Count Dracula laugh.

Mandy and I tried desperately to escape his grip, but realizing there was no escape, we groaned, rolled our eyes at each other, took a deep breath, and waited for the bomb to go off. We burst out laughing just as Mark let 'er rip and ended up getting more than he bargained for. He actually sharted right there in the street. Mandy and I couldn't even stand up we were laughing so hard. With that much dead weight pulling on him, Mark let go and dropped to his knees too. He was laughing too, but I got the feeling he was a little embarrassed as well. As we girls rolled in laughter in the grass by the sidewalk, Mark crawled behind the tree, and we saw his hand reach out and pull back with a fist full of dried leaves.

"You're lucky it's fall, Mr. Poopy Pants," I mocked, dropping over again, tears rolling down my face as I clutched my belly and gasped for air between roars of laughter.

CHAPTER SIX

"Hurry! Faster! They're gaining on you." I whispered as I sped down the dirt road, the man and his wagon rapidly approaching behind me. *Maybe he hasn't seen me*, I hoped as I quickly darted into the tall grass along the side of the road. Once in the grass, I froze like a statue, hoping the man and his wagon would just pass me by. As they approached, I noticed there were no women in the back of the wagon. *He's alone*, I thought, just as I saw the familiar old farmhouse in the distance. *If only I could get to that house, maybe I could call for help. The girls need me.*

I let the wagon get about one hundred yards down the road and then sneaked out of the grass. As I came out of my cover, I made sure the man was not looking back. When I was sure the coast was clear, I took off at a dead run for the house. "Please, God, let there be a phone," I prayed out loud, pumping my arms and legs as fast as I could.

Gasping for breath, I turned my head just in time to see the man look in my direction as I rounded the corner of the old house. Not knowing if he saw me or not, I grabbed the doorknob and burst into the house. "Where is it? Where is it? Come on, there has to be one," I heard myself say as I searched in vain for a telephone.

"Come out here, my dear. I know you're in there." I could hear him dragging something on the siding of the house as he made his way around. I startled as he appeared in a window close to where I was hiding and whispered, "Silly girl, you know you can't hide from me, and no one will believe your tall tales. It is no secret to anyone that you have a very active imagination." I sucked into the wall as tightly as I could and silence pounded in my ears as he moved away from the window. In a few seconds, I could hear the front porch stairs creak and moan as he ascended them, making his way toward the front door. The large, broken screen door burst open, and the man shouted into the room, "Now, don't make me wait. You know how I hate to wait for what I want."

I could hear him wandering around the house talking, all the while trying to coax me out of my hiding spot. *Hold your breath, hold your breath,* I said to myself, looking around the room for an escape. Just then, I noticed a door at the end of the hall that seemed to drop into the earth. I had to risk it. I sat silently listening, not breathing, trying to get a fix on the man's position. When I thought I'd heard him at the other end of the house, I made a run for it. Reaching the door, I took the stairs two at a time.

Descending into the darkness, I felt a sudden surge of energy as I remembered that there was a flashlight in my backpack. Stopping only for a second, I dropped my bag on the next step above me and dug it out. "Please work. You have to work," I begged as I grabbed the cold metal object lying at the bottom of my bag. As I switched the on button, I was grateful to have my new surrounding blessedly illuminated. "Thank you, God," I said out loud as I panned the light along the walls of this dungeon.

When I finally looked down, I realized that I was actually standing on a floor and not a stair. That's when something registered in my brain. I lifted the light back up to one of the walls and discovered that what I thought was a window was actually a dark hole dug into the dirt where the wall had actually been removed. My heart raced as I darted for the hole. I leapt through the opening, making my way as fast as I could, deeper and deeper into the tunnel, not knowing where it would come out or if it would just come to an end but knowing wherever it was, it was in the opposite direction of the man.

Rounding a turn, I felt my legs begin to burn just as they did when we were running hills in practice. I must have been on an uphill climb. My mind raced, *Where is this taking me? Oh, my God, my legs are going to fall off.* Gasping for breath and feeling, I suddenly felt relieved and free, for in front of me was a set of doors. "I made it," I said to myself as I reached for the latch and simultaneously shut off my flashlight.

"What the heck?" I said out loud as light from somewhere on the other side came shining through the slit between the doors, showing me a completely unfamiliar latch mechanism. For some sinister reason, someone had tied it shut with tons of fishing line. Panic began to set in, and tears were on the edge of my eyelids. I didn't have any idea how I was going to get this mess untangled. I kept thinking, *Why didn't you put that pocketknife in your pack like Dad said to? You idiot!*

Pacing the hallway, a figure outside the door caused a shadow to appear on the walls as it passed the crack between the doors where the light was coming from. I stopped talking and froze. Who could it be? My mind raced as I tried to figure out if I should turn and go back the way I came or try to undo the knot and hope the person was someone who could help me. As I brooded over my situation, something grabbed my shoulder. I screamed, only to find my mom standing over me.

"Sami, wake up! What are you doing in our room again? You're thirteen. Don't you think it's about time you stop sleeping on our floor?" my mom said, letting go of my shoulder, unable to hide the frustration in her voice.

"Sorry, Mom, I didn't even know I was in here. Did you hear me come in? What time is it?"

"No, but I heard you screaming just now. That scares me to death every time you do that. What is scaring you so badly? Maybe I need to make an appointment for you to see a doctor."

"No. What the heck is a doctor supposed to do?" I quickly interrupted.

"But you're too old to be sleeping in here. This has to stop, and it's really startling to wake up to you screaming right by my head." She paused, took a breath, and slid off the bed to sit next to me on the floor. "Is it the same dream every time? Can you remember it at all?"

"Usually it's the same people and place, but the story and situation changes," I replied. "And no, I don't normally remember the details, just that it scares me," I lied.

Mom touched my hair and said, "Could it be because of the girls at school? Is Becky up to her old tricks again?" She let her hand drop and pulled her pajamas down over her knees then added, "I know you try to not let them bother you, but maybe it does more than you think, and maybe it's coming out in your dream." She paused again for a second then added, "What do you think?"

"I don't know," I said, getting up and scooping my blankets, pillow, and two stuffed animals into my arms. I headed for the door, paying no attention to any more of her questions.

As I walked down the hall, I told myself that I knew exactly what the cause was, or should I say, who, and it wasn't a girl. I couldn't tell her. Years ago, I was given a warning that if I ever told anyone, not only would I be considered a bad girl and get taken away, but sent to a place where I didn't know anybody until I died. I didn't want to get taken away or die. I have to stop this nightmare or at the very least find a way to keep from ending up on my parents' floor.

Entering my room, I came up with a plan. "I know," I uttered out loud to myself. "Maybe if I work out twice as hard, that will make me so exhausted that I'll be too tired to dream anything." Silly as it seemed, I made a pact with myself. And as I saw my own reflection in the bathroom mirror I said, "That's it…starting today."

CHAPTER SEVEN

Fall and spring seemed to be when I had the most trouble sleeping. My stomach ached and I caught every bug that swooped around me. So far, this year wasn't any different than any of the others I had experienced. In order to escape my memories, during fall sports, I pushed myself to the limit running in the morning before school, running cross country practice after school, lifting weights after practice, and then hitting an aerobics class at the community center before running the miles home. This worked perfectly. I was so tired by the end of the day that I didn't have time to think. And as an added bonus, for some reason the more I worked out, the less I ate, which when put all together, literally added up to an exhausted, sixty-five-pound, walking stick-person with muscles that succeeded in sleeping like a baby. This was my way of playing "hard to want." I mean really, who would want to touch a person who looked like death warmed over. *An attractive thought if I do say so myself.* "Perfect." In between my chuckles, I whispered, totally proud of myself, "Works for me."

After years of practice, I was the master at keeping secrets. No one even noticed what I was doing to myself. Hey, the gymnastics coaches loved it. I was a fourteen-year-old girl who was built and looked like a ten-year-old boy with strong, lanky muscles, and, after hanging out with my brother and his buddies all these years, a total Kamikaze.

One problem: Wisconsin got so cold in December that your breath could practically freeze in midair. That made running outside not the most desirable activity and one for which vanity must be tossed out the window. For example, not only does your hair get mashed by your stocking cap, but your eyes water, and your nose runs faster than your legs, which over time causes the snot to freeze right into the peach fuzz of your upper lip. These attractive features that grace the faces of those who endure the frozen tundra are affectionately known in the Midwest as snot sickles. *Gross.* I might look like something from the "Bodies in Motion" science exhibit our class saw on a field trip to the Twin Cities, but I didn't want to be one with frozen snot stuck to my upper lip. Not only were they sick and nasty, but when they melt, they taste like salty crap. Yep, there was no way around it; I'd have to pour myself even deeper into gymnastics. *No problem. It's not like I have a life anyway.*

I discovered that I loved gymnastics even more than I first thought I would. Everything went great until I started progressing super fast, passing all but a couple of girls who had been on the team for years. And, oh yeah, I think I forgot to mention that Becky's sister, Maggie, convinced her that she should go out for gymnastics too. I didn't care. I just buried myself in deep and tried with everything in me to ignore her jabs and outright nastiness as much as possible. However, when I started learning things way faster than she did, let's just say the green-eyed monster came out in full force.

With Becky at practice, I had my work cut out for me to get time on the equipment. She would talk crap about me behind my back to the girls as usual and get them to go along with her garbage. Most nights, I would stay after everyone left with either my coach or one of my guy friends and practice. Her big thing was to talk everyone into hoarding me off the equipment. Even though we were all supposed to take turns and wait in line, someone would inevitably run up to whatever we were working on and jump in my spot. This happened all the time. It really pissed me off that coach never said or did anything about it. I knew she had to have noticed; no one can be that big of a moron.

About six weeks into the season when I was leaving the gym, the basketball players where in the hall screwing around and attempting to suck the water fountain dry. Seeing all those boys made me sick to my stomach. Shock registered in my brain when what Becky said in the locker room that first day of school about my chest or lack thereof, came into my mind like a jolt of lightning. It took everything in me not to turn around and run back into the gym, especially since Becky and her buddies were in the mix of boys, loving the fact that they were wearing nothing but leotards. *Sick. They're all nasty.*

Stopping dead in my tracks, I instantly brought my hands up to conceal as much of my wannabe nubby boobs as possible. Picking at my right palm, pretending I was pulling off a torn callus, I put my head down and pressed on, desperately not wanting to be noticed. Wishful thinking on my part. The slutty girls on our team had the boys so wound up a speck of lint would have been noticed in that crowd. Oh how I wished to not be in a leotard but part of the tile on the wall.

Slowly and cautiously I approached the circle of chaos. Instantly, a couple of the boys saw me and tried to block my path. Thank God for Darren Jonas III, my best guy friend in school. He was huge, six-feet-four inches tall, and two hundred pounds of pure muscle. I'm pretty sure even the big floppy ears that flanked his closely set jade-green eyes and shaved head had muscles, which made him a little hard to look at. Mark teased that he had a face for radio. That's not quite how my dad described someone who was a little on the not attractive side. Every time he'd see DJ, my dad would always say, "That boy is uglier than the remnants of a frog after five minutes in a microwave. Good thing he's a nice kid…hard worker too. That's a good thing, 'cause it's the only way he's catching himself a wife."

It's always good to know someone like DJ. He watched out for me. It was kind of like "Puny and the Beast" whenever we would hang out. As I tried to get past the two dorks blocking my way, DJ came to my rescue. Grabbing me around the waist from behind, he whispered in my ear that it was him and that he'd get me out of there. Without even so much as a grunt, he swept me up over his head like a paper doll. If you calculate his arm length, I must have been at least seven and a half feet in the air. No one could touch me there. It was awesome!

Laughing half out of embarrassment and half because it was fun flying that high in the air, I shouted over the hooting and hollering, "Thanks for the lift, bud. You rock!"

As he sat me down, he was grinning from ear to ear and laughing right along with me. "What do you weigh, about fifty?" he said and tried to flip the little turd-shaped ponytail I was attempting to grow.

"Ha ha, I wish." I smiled back, swatting his hand away from my head. "You picked me up like it was nothing." After thinking a second, I added, "Hey, you should come up and let me teach you how to spot the tricks I learned all summer in the cities at club. Maybe then I could get some real practice time."

I could practically see the steam coming out of his ears after what I'd suggested finally sunk in. Angrily he said, "What's the deal, Bec and her groupie sluts pushing you out and hogging equipment?"

Pulling on his arm to get him to walk out of the hallway with me, I rolled my eyes and answered, "How'd you guess?"

He turned to head into the boys' locker room but stopped at the top of the stairs and said to me, "Those wenches need to be taught a lesson. Can you stay late tomorrow after practice?"

Smiling, I yelled back, "Yeah, why?" I already knew what he was thinking by the impish smirk he was flashing at me, with one eyebrow raised stepped back toward him, saying, "I know that look. You have a plan?"

"I do, madam," he said, walking away, twisting to look back at me, letting out a deep, sinister laugh.

Shaking my head, I laughed and headed across the gym to the locker room Mandy and I used for cross-country. With all the other winter girls' athletes in the main locker room, I had blissful peace and solitude down in my little "hole-in-the-wall" under the stage.

CHAPTER EIGHT

The next day, I couldn't wait for school to end to see what DJ had in store. Knowing him, I knew it was going to be good. He was exceptionally talented in the dark art of evil sabotage.

The day felt like it lasted forever, but when the time finally came for practice, I raced to the locker room and changed quickly. Slipping on my last sock, I bolted out the door, up the stairs, and through the smelly gym, weaving my way through basketball players. Turning the corner and sprinting down the hall toward our gymnastics room, I remembered that DJ wasn't coming until the end. "Slow down, silly," I heard myself say. "Save some of that energy for the good stuff."

All during practice, I kept waiting for something to happen. But my so-called teammates were at their finest today…budging in line so I didn't get as many turns and talking crap when I actually got to go just loud enough for me to hear. As usual, no one had the guts to say anything to my face or stand up to Miss Becky. Everyone has a pet peeve, and mine is being ignored. I hate that almost more than anything else in the world; Becky knew it and didn't ever hold back on an opportunity to use it against me.

I don't know why I expected things to be any different. Maybe it was because I finally had what I considered a positive secret… or because I knew I actually had a plan up my sleeve to get to work on some of the new tricks I learned at club this summer. I don't know, but my bubble was sure burst when I was smacked in the face with the reality that I had no one to share it with. I wished Mandy was a gymnast or that Dani hadn't gotten sick. Maybe she could have turned some of that chub into muscle. Smiling to myself at the thought of my sick friend in a leotard, my odd brain wasted no time in making me realize and snicker at the fact that we would both be bald…everywhere. If I ever lost control of my verbal filter and started blurting out what I was really thinking, they would have locked me up.

With only a couple of minutes of practice left, I slinked out the back doors of our gym. I took a quick left and bolted down the hall. My mom's first-grade classroom was buried deep in the far west corner of the building and completely deserted this time of day. Bless my mom; she always kept a secret stash of black leotards in her closet for me to change into, and luckily the little kids got their own bathroom right in the room. For some reason, I had this problem when every time I hit the springboard or tumbled, I peed just enough to be noticeable. I couldn't even imagine what Becky and her wenches would have done with that one.

After I changed into yet another black leotard, I glanced up at the clock on my way out of mom's room. *Yes, it's almost five thirty.* In about thirty seconds, I sneaked back into the gym and made my way across the gym unnoticed. *Where is DJ?* I wondered as I once again waited in silence for my turn on the beam. Just then, Coach yelled for us to hit the locker room, and everyone bolted out of the room like their pants were on fire. I slapped my hands, causing chalk to create an opaque fog in front of my face. As the smoke cleared, in came DJ, sweaty from basketball practice, and the huge smile on his face could not even begin to mask his aroma.

Catching up to his stink next to me and slamming his fists to his hips, he grinned and said, "Okay, Mouse, teach me."

"What are you talking about?" I asked.

DJ flexed his muscles and whispered loudly, "Teach me to spot you. My plan is to see you totally kick all of their butts from here to kingdom come. They think they can keep you down by keeping you off the equipment? Well, they'd better think again 'cause you and me are gonna bust it until they can only dream of catching you. How sweet it will be to make those green-eyed, two-faced hags wish they'd never heard of gymnastics."

"Well. Look at you all puffed up with all the answers. Dude, I'm in. Let's do it." And with that, we went to work. Every night, he secretly met me in the gym after everyone else left, and we put in a couple of hours jumping, twisting, falling, swinging, and laughing again and again. Over and over we'd practice 'till I could barely move and had no skin left on my hands. It was awesome! He could literally throw me around like a roll of toilet paper; I never had to worry about being dropped on my head. He just had to duck a lot so I didn't kick him.

Pretty sure I sprained every finger and toe on one part of his body or another, but he never let go, no matter what. And when I say no matter what, that's exactly what I mean. Even though he mastered the art of giving me snuggies by grabbing my leo if he couldn't get a hold of a limb, we both got over the blushing when my butt cheeks would hang out as I dangled in the air from his huge hands. The only time I ever got embarrassed and cringed was when after placing me gently on my feet by the back of my leo, he dropped to his knees, grabbing his crotch, moaning as if death were imminent and probably preferred. Unfortunately more for him than me, this wasn't a one-time event. It never changed; every time I crashed into his balls, it took me awhile to be able to look him in the face again.

On occasion, DJ did manage to get his revenge for my misplaced hits. When he'd reach in to catch me and instead of getting a hold of my leo, he'd accidentally smack me in the chest. Not only did that hurt, but I always felt amazingly stupid as to the lack of squish that should have been present and accounted for. I knew the nubby, little marble-like protrusions under my skin had to make him wonder if I was truly from this planet. In the end, it didn't matter. He saved my butt. And we were both getting better every day, one exciting, exhilarating, embarrassing, silly moment after another.

Even though we were making tons of progress, it didn't come without a price. Some of the crashes we took made us both think twice about whether it was all worth it or not. In the end, my "Evel Knievel" work ethic always won, and I wasn't going to shy away from anything just because it scared me. DJ knew this and was right there with me.

One late January night, when DJ and I were about to start working, he looked at me and said, "So, Mighty Mouse, what's the plan for today?"

Turning to look around the gym, I smiled sheepishly and answered, "The vault's out. You feel like taking one in the gonads for me tonight?"

"Anything for the right cause, my little friend." He gulped exaggeratedly. "Even sterility." With that he punched me in the arm, proceeded to pull his pants up around his chest, and added, "Besides, after seeing you in the hall today between science and math, I knew something was up. You had the 'look,' so I put on my titanium cup tonight."

Trying to blow off his last comment, I tried to stifle my laughter and headed to the end of the vaulting strip. Walking backward to the other end of the gym, I yelled, "I'll tell you about my idea in a minute. Let me take a couple of warm-ups…and you should probably get your pants out of your tonsils. That's my look."

When I got to my takeoff mark at the end of the room, I shouted, "Hey, D, stand in the middle of the landing mat and see if you can measure how high I am."

"Why?" he shouted back as he stepped up onto the mat.

"I'll explain in a sec. See if you can get your hands on my back as I go over your head. Make sure you aim for my hips and not my upper back. And don't push, just measure."

"Okay, Okay! You're awful bossy," I heard him say as I bolted toward him on a dead run.

Hitting the springboard at full speed, I reached up with my hands and drove my heels to the ceiling as hard as I could. As soon as I felt the soft leather of the horse contact my hands, I blocked my shoulders with all my might. Up, up I went. It felt like I floated forever. I didn't even feel DJ's hands graze my leo. As I descended to the mat, I knew it was the big vault I wanted.

Grabbing my hips on the landing, DJ gasped, "Holy crap, Mouse, I couldn't even reach you on my tippy toes. What's up with that?"

"Well, my giant friend, I learned a new vault at club last summer and have been trying to get my nerve up all season to try it without a pit," I said, motioning for him to sit by me on the stack of folded mats that were kept at the end of the vault landing. "Have a seat, and I'll explain."

As he sat down beside me, I could see the excitement beginning to stir in his eyes as he realized what I had in mind. "You're going to pull a front flip out of that handspring like those girls on TV do, aren't you?" He spit out.

"Yep." I said matter-of-factly. "You up for it?"

"Yeah, woman! How do I not let you die?" he asked.

"Wait here," I said as I stood and started across the gym to where the coach keeps her notebook and pencil. "I'll draw it out for you first, then we'll move the giant gush mats behind the horse so you're higher and I get a softer landing."

I snatched the pad and pencil off the stereo stand and jogged quickly back to where he was sitting. As I illustrated the new vault, I talked DJ through it and demonstrated how he was to spot me.

After about ten minutes of discussion and practicing timers on the floor, I asked, "You ready, big guy?"

He smiled and said, "You bet. Don't chicken out. I don't know where the janitor keeps his mop and bucket, and I think I'd probably have a lot of explaining to do if there's a dead body and blood all over the gymnastics room tomorrow."

"Relax, when have I ever chickened on you?" I said over my shoulder as I headed to the other end of the gym.

Learning new tricks was one of those adventures that neither of us was ever sure what the first try would bring. When I reached my starting position, I took a big breath, shook my head, stretched for a second, and let the Kamikaze in me take over. Running as hard as I could, totally focused on the mission at hand, hitting the springboard perfectly, and nailing my block off the horse, I had enough extra height to complete the entire rotation into the gush mats. However, on this on particular occasion, it became very obvious why the gymnasts on TV separate their knees to the sides of their bodies as they rotate. I rotated, landed on my butt, and froze.

Stumbling backwards off the mat, DJ shouted, "Oh, my God, Sam, That was awesome!" That no sooner got out of his mouth than he noticed how I was sitting and that I hadn't moved. "You're not moving?" He said as he stepped toward me. "What's up?" I could feel him staring at me, so I slowly peeled both knees from where they were lodged in my eye sockets and turned my head toward him.

"Wow, that's gonna leave a mark," he said, clasping his hand over his mouth and trying not to laugh.

"Shut up—really?" I said, trying to be serious, still not moving from my spot on the mat, searching my face with both hands. "Dude, I can't feel my face."

Shaking his head, he said, "Girl, you're gonna soon enough."

I let out a huge sigh and flopped to my back on the mat. DJ couldn't hold it anymore; he dove onto the mat next to me, and we both laughed until we were bawling. I could feel my eyes growing puffier by the second, and the tears of laughter didn't help the pain.

After we settled down a little, I stared at the ceiling and said, "No way I can come to school tomorrow. Bec and the girls will have a field day with this one."

"Screw them. Tell 'em they should see the other guy." He laughed and got up from the mat. "You need to get ice on that before you look like an alien." Walking over to where he threw his stuff, he yelled back to me, "Lucky for you I happen to have an ice pack right here in my gym bag." When he got to his bag, he gave it a kick and it flopped open. He reached down and pulled out the little, white, plastic pouch and headed back toward me.

Punching it with his fist to activate the chemicals inside, he gave it a shake and tossed it at me. "Here, black-eyed Susie. You look so hot right now. I can hardly contain myself."

I took the icepack and lovingly placed it across my eyes. "Wow, that's a little bit of heaven right there," I said.

After about twenty minutes, DJ said, "You ready to try that again or what?" Grabbing the ice pack from me, he shook it and said, "This is warm anyway. Come on, let's get this show on the road."

We worked for another hour before calling it a night. I walked away from that particular practice looking like I'd gone twenty-two rounds with Mike Tyson. Needless to say, after that day, I always pulled my knees apart no matter how goofy I thought it looked. But hey, that's how the two of us worked. We thought of it, tried it, and kept trying it until I got it right. Talk about a couple of total nut cases, alone in a dark gym, crashing and burning and growing ever more skilled in the process.

With DJ and me working so hard, it wasn't long before I took a varsity spot away from one of the older girls. Needless to say, this made me even more popular among the girls. Just when I thought it couldn't get any worse, all hell broke loose. Practice was nearly unbearable. I'd go home every night and cry myself to sleep. All of this because of one stupid freak…me.

For the rest of the season, I continued to push myself to the breaking point, pouring every ounce of energy I had into practice and doing my best at ignoring the garbage that was going on around me. It was the only way to get past the evil. When would it end? I had to survive…keep pushing, keep pushing. It will all go away. That's how I seemed to handle everything. It was working; why change?

CHAPTER NINE

By the end of that first season, I was exhausted, but I'd accomplished something that had eluded every gymnast in my school before me. I qualified and placed at the state meet as a seventh-grade, first-year athlete. But not without a price…the girls in my school were horrid, and they didn't like the fact that I'd found a way around their games, which made the harassment worse than ever.

One Friday afternoon in late April, as I was coming out of band, my brother, a drummer, grabbed my arm, concern showing in his eyes, "Hey, Sam, you want me to walk you home? I heard Becky and some of her loser friends talking about you in the hall at lunch, and let's just say that it might be best if you have an escort. It sounded to me as if she's up to her old tricks again. She needs to get a life."

"No kidding. What the heck did I ever do to those guys?" I said, putting my flute on the shelf and turning to look him in the face.

"Kicked their butt. Duh," he said, winking at me and giving me one of his mischievous little grins and a brotherly shove.

Punching him in the arm, I added, "Good thing their butts are so big. I'd hate to miss."

"If you missed those giant badonkadonks, even I'd make fun of you," Mark's friend, Joe, said, poking his head and eventually his body in between us. "Did I hear someone mention raging hippos in heat? Hey, I bet the smell is about the same." Laughing at his own joke, Joe started to moo. Everyone around was laughing at his bad joke. It was great because a bunch of the guys chimed in to the slamming party we were having at Becky and her little posse's expense.

Anytime I hear people talking crap about the mean girls, I find it comforting to know I'm not the only one who thinks they suck. It was a great way to end a school day.

On the way home, Mark and I continued our trash talk about the nasty girls for a few blocks. As we were entering the alley behind Becky's house, Mark could tell something had just sent a chill down my spine.

Reassuringly, he said, "Relax, nothing's gonna happen. They wouldn't dare do anything when I'm here."

"I know, but they still make me nervous."

"You worked hard for all those bulging muscles. Don't you know how to use them for anything but flying through the air upside down?" he asked, giving my bicep a hard squeeze.

"How would I know any self-defense, you dork? The only thing I ever fight with is you...and I do mean 'thing,' literally," I said jokingly.

Smacking me on the back of the head and jumping away before I retaliated, he added, "Come on, tough guy. When we get home I'll show you some—." Suddenly, he stopped talking and squinted toward our house. The next thing I knew, I was practically flying down the alley as he grabbed my arm and began to run toward our house. I would never have been able to keep up if he hadn't had a hold of me, as he was one of the fastest guys in our school. It was so much fun to just relax and let my legs go. I loved this and thought he was still trying to lighten up the mood by getting me out of this alley as quickly as possible. That's when I saw it. Something was swinging in the wind in front of my bedroom window.

As we approached our house, the figure came into focus, and I gasped when I saw that hanging from a noose was a ratty, old doll, stripped naked. Walking across the yard, neither of us said a word. It was covered with vulgar, threatening messages; it had an arm and a leg missing, and its bland, yellow hair was matted and sticking up all over.

Mark stopped in front of my window and growled, "Now she's gone too far. This is seriously sick. She isn't going to get away with this. I won't let her threaten you like this. No way I'm letting another monster in your face. All this time, I thought she was just talk, but this is way psycho. You go in. Mom's home. I'll be back in a bit."

"Where you going?" I asked, concerned he was about to do something stupid. "Don't worry about it," he snapped.

As soon as I went in the house, Mark disappeared on his bike. Just after dark, I heard a car in the driveway. Nervous that maybe he'd gone to the police, I jumped off my bed and darted to the window. I had to know what was going on. Luckily, the trees weren't totally covered in leaves, and I could see the driveway from my bedroom. From my perch on top of my dresser, I could see Joe Turner's decked-out, spotless, red GTO. I swear he should marry that car he loves it so much. He polishes it more than he showers.

I hopped off my dresser when I heard my brother thumping down the stairs. I could tell by the loud thumping that he was obviously in a hurry and skipping stairs on the way down. I figured he was heading to his room until he came busting into my room out of breath shouting, "Get your coat, Mouse. We're on a mission! This is gonna be great!"

As I reached for my hooded sweatshirt, he grabbed my arm, and laughed. "You're going to love this. Hurry up!"

"Where are we going?" I asked, knowing this couldn't be good.

"You'll see. Just move it. We're gonna show that psycho that she can't threaten people and get away with it." He was laughing excitedly as we hurriedly left the house and piled into Joe's baby.

"Wow, Joe, your car reeks. What the heck? Kinda smells like your girlfriend," I said, grinning and grabbing my nose to stop any more of the nasty smell from entering and probably burning my nasal passages.

Laughing a sinister laugh and starting his car, he answered my question with the only answer that fit the moment, "It is crap, little mousey girl, and soon it will be warm and flying." Still confused, I just looked at him, shook my head, and laughed.

Traveling past Becky's house, I flipped off the structure behind the seat, thinking no one saw me. I was wrong. Seth, Joe's twin brother, saw me and said, "She needs to be taught a lesson. They've been nasty to you for far too long already. We've all had enough." Relaxing back in his seat and putting his hands behind his head, he laid his head back and sat quietly with a grin.

Approximately two blocks down the street from Becky Miles's house, we pulled into an alley behind an old house everyone said was haunted. It was a giant, two-story, Victorian-style house that had been abandoned years ago. Most of the windows had been boarded up ever since old Larry Becker shot himself in the kitchen. Rumor has it creepy old Larry's ghost still waits in that room to scare away trespassers. I've always been too scared to go in, but those who have don't ever do it again.

When Joe turned into the driveway of the old house, I made sure they all knew exactly how I felt. "Ah, come on," I said. I leaned forward from the backseat to get a better look at the raggedy old building through the windshield. "I'm not going in there, guys. No way!"

"Come on, Sam. You don't believe that crap, do you? We've all been in there tons of times and lived to tell about it," my brother said, getting out of the passenger's side door.

Giving me a nudge to get out of the car, Seth added, "Don't worry. It's not haunted. That's just an old rumor started by old people to scare the kids away so they don't party in there and trash the place."

Joe opened my car door and said, "You've never been a wuss before, don't start now, Sami." He reached in, grabbed my hand, and pulled me gently out of the car. "Come on, would we ever let anything happen to you?" He winked.

By the time I was finally out of Joe's beloved automobile, the other two boys were already entering through a broken basement window. I was so scared I could feel the bile rising in my throat. This was almost as bad as my nightmare. I got to the window and knelt down to look in.

"Oh my gosh, what have you dorks gotten me into now? We're so going to be in trouble if we get caught," I protested as I slid my skinny frame through the window.

As I landed on the basement floor, a putrid odor hit my nose, and I gagged. "What is that stench?" I asked, trying to hold my breath. "Is that the rotting, leftover remains of old Larry?" Moving back toward the window, I shouted, "Get me out of here right now!"

"Crap," Joe said matter-of-factly.

"What?" I asked, turning back to Joe.

"It's crap. Come on, I know you know what that smells like. You live with him don't you?" he added, pointing at Mark.

Turning back to face them with my hands on my hips I said, "Okay, come on, I know you guys do some sick and disgusting stuff, but you really don't take dumps in this place, do you?"

"Don't be dumb. I know you've witnessed us expressing our en-thusiasm for our unbelievably awesome bodily functions, but this mission needs the special touch none of us could supply…at the time anyway," Seth boasted, puffing up his chest and grinning that naughty grin again.

"Hey, where did Mark go?" I asked, looking around the large, open space.

"I'm right here, Mouse. And I come bearing gifts," he said, ap-pearing from around a corner to our left. He was holding out what looked like a giant piece of wadded-up tinfoil. It looked like a dou-ble-sized Jiffy Pop popcorn maker.

"Scary?" I asked as he handed me the present. "This obviously isn't popcorn, big brother. It smells like there's a dead animal in it or something." Pushing it back at him, I shook my head and said, "No thanks. Please, you keep it. Really, I insist." Taking back the smelly package, Mark pealed apart a section of the foil exposing the contents inside. As soon as the silver pieces separated, the world's most disgustingly foul aroma erupted into the room.

"Whoa, and I thought it stunk before!" I yelled, grabbing for my nose.

"It's crap." Seth smiled. "Compliments of several of our dad's cows."

"Do you have any idea how long it takes to find a perfect pile like this?" Mark proudly added. "And we did it all for you." He continued shoving the poop in my face like I was supposed to be totally grateful.

"Why on earth would you guys want that much cow manure? That's just sick and wrong," I stated, giving my brother and his gross friends a look of absolute confusion and disgust. Actually, I had to admit, it was pretty funny, and I had a sneaking suspicion this little package might just be a present for Becky Miles.

"Watch and learn, little sister," Joe said as he took the smelly, poo-filled tinfoil from Mark and placed it into a big brown paper grocery bag as gently as if it were an extremely fragile glass figurine. Once he had it perfectly settled at the bottom of the bag, he looked around and yelled to Seth, "Hey, dude, go find me some paper for kindling." Just then, my light bulb went on, and I knew exactly what's about to take place and who the recipient of the present was to be. Excitement bubbled up in me at the prospect of getting a little even for the disturbing, hanging victim left at my window. Joy and exhilaration took over, and I forgot all about how scary this house was suppose to be. Dying to help, I burst out laughing and ran around like a crazy person in search of anything that would burn and burn quickly, for this fire was to be a little, sweet revenge.

Once the kindling was in place, Joe carefully rolled down the top of the bag and yelled, "Voila, the masterpiece is complete, my friends! It's time to initiate the attack." With that, he scooped up the bag into his arms, and we all followed him back out the window and into the alley.

"Okay, Mouse, follow close, stay quiet, and keep down. Got it?" Mark whispered as we walked side by side down the weedy, graveled path.

"Yep, got it," I whispered back.

Approaching the end of the alley, Mark turned to me and pointed at a thick row of honeysuckle bushes that lined the street directly across from and facing Becky's house. The owner, Mr. Madsen, planted this thick, creepy, green fence of foliage around the entire yard years ago. As luck would have it, the Madsens always left for Arizona in the winter and hadn't returned from their vacation yet. "You're going to be the lookout. Crouch down and hide behind the bushes. We'll be back in two seconds. If you see any cars, whistle two short blasts so we can duck out of sight. Any questions?"

"Nope. I'm good," I guaranteed him as I sneaked away from them and assumed my position as guard in the bushes.

From between the leaves I could see the three commandos stealthily making their way to the target with Seth leading the way, Joe in the middle carrying the package, and Mark bringing up the rear. Becky's house was one of those houses that started out little and as the family grew, more and more additions were built on to accommodate. Actually, every time they had a kid, they built another level on top. To be honest, I'm not sure what style you'd actually call it. If I had to label it, I'd probably say an old country house because it was white and had lots of little windows and a giant porch that encircled it. Six steps led up to the porch and as the boys crept up them, I could see their heads craning in every direction, searching for any sign of life. When they reached the top, they carefully crawled across the wooden planks that led to the front door. I could see Joe gingerly place the bag a few inches from the door. Mark dug something out of his pocket and handed it to him. It had to be a lighter, I thought, and I couldn't help but giggle to myself. Joe reached his arm forward, touching the bag, and within seconds I could see a flame erupt. As soon as the fire started, Seth rang the doorbell, and they all leaped over the side railing and sprinted as if their lives depended on it across the street toward my hiding spot. It was only a matter of seconds until they all flew around the end of the hedge and bolted for a place to watch the excitement.

Out of breath, Mark asked in a low whisper, "Anyone answer the door yet?"

"It's just cracking open now," I whispered back. "Watch, watch, watch. Here someone comes."

We all held fast and watched through the leaves as Becky's dad, a huge, dark-haired man with an unruly, thick beard, opened the door. Seeing the fire, he yelled something back inside the house, turned back to the flames, and instantly began stomping on the conflagration with all his might. As his third stomp hit the bag, manure went sailing into the air. It was beautiful because the rest of the family (Becky in the lead) came rushing out onto the porch just in time to get totally plastered with a "manure shower." As the poo flew, we could see huge globs of manure smack Becky right in the face just as she screamed. She was spitting and sputtering, just making it to the railing as she began to blow chunks right into her mom's favorite rose bushes. From our hiding spots, we were fist pounding each other like crazy and trying desperately to stay quiet, but that was way too good.

Looking back through the bushes, I turned quickly back to the boys, placed my index finger to my mouth, and whispered as quietly as I possible, "Shhh! Her dad is coming down the steps, and he definitely doesn't look like he just won the Publisher's Clearing House giveaway."

"Come on! Let's get out of here," Joe whispered back as he waved his right hand in the air, indicating for us to all follow.

"I don't want to go. It's entirely too much fun watching Miss Becky suffer for once," I said through my whispered giggles as I turned back to pull the leaves apart for another look.

"We can gloat back at the car," he whispered, grabbing my arm, pulling me in his direction. "We have to get out of here before they call the cops." I reluctantly followed.

Keeping low, Joe in the lead, we sneaked right down to where the hedge of bushes turned a right angle and led across the front yard. We stayed down and intertwined with them as best we could. Looking back, I could see her dad stomping around his front yard, wiping his feet as he walked. Becky, her mom, and her sister were standing in the grass to the right of the porch, trying to spray off the manure with the outdoor hose.

Seth whispered from somewhere ahead of us, "That has to be freezing."

Actually, I was thinking the same thing, but the most gratifying part was that it was only April, and the temperature was in the low forties. Laughing to myself, I noticed the boys were gleefully all taking part in the celebration too as we weaved our way through the trees and shrubs congesting all the front and backyards on our way to the haunted house.

As we got into Joe's car to leave, we all dove in, Joe fired up the engine, and we were out of there.

"Thanks, you guys," I said. "That was so worth the trip." Sitting back in my seat I added, "Oh man, did you see the look on Becky's face when that first glob smacked her right in the mouth? That was perfect."

"I wonder if she swallowed any. That would rock! Serves her right," Joe said from the driver's seat.

"I've known she's full of crap for a long time." I joked.

"It's about time she got a little of her own medicine." Pride and satisfaction showed in Mark's voice as he turned toward the backseat so I could see his face too.

"Maybe she'll mellow out for a while now," Seth said.

Turning to look at me in the back from his position in the driver's seat, Joe said, "If not, you let us know. We'll be right there for ya, Mouse."

I was so touched by how the guys stood up for me tonight and risked getting into a ton of trouble that I didn't know what to say. I knew Mark had always been there for me, but his friends hadn't ever done anything like that for me before. So I just looked down at the newly mudded-up floor mats and grinned, "Thanks a lot, guys. That really was awesome ...and totally fun too."

When I got in the house, the phone was ringing. It was DJ. I wasn't surprised to hear his voice. He lives in the house next to Becky's and can see her porch from his bedroom window.

"Hey, did you see the fire at the Becky's house?"

"What fire?" I lied.

"It was totally awesome! Her front porch was on fire and her dad stomped it out with his foot right in front of Becky, her mom, and her sister. I think some fire sprayed up on them 'cause they all ran off the porch and sprayed each other with the freezing cold water from their hose," he said at mach twelve. "You should have heard them screaming. I was laughing my butt off. And her dad, wow was he mad. I wonder if he burned his feet or something. He was stomping all over yard like he was still trying to put out the fire."

"Sounds like fun," I said, obviously not hiding my giddiness about the whole situation well enough. DJ can always tell when I'm totally full of it.

"You dog, what'd you do?" DJ pleaded. I could tell by his voice he knew something was up and that I knew way more than I was saying.

Putting on my best innocent voice, I questioned, "Who? Me?"

"Come on, Mouse, spill it. I want to have some fun at Becky's expense too. Pretty sure you owe me that." I could hear the smile in his voice as he begged me to tell him what really happened.

"It wasn't me. I swear, but I watched from the Madsens' honeysuckles across the street," I stated with obvious satisfaction in my voice. "…and it wasn't ash or fire or anything like that that they were washing off themselves. Much better and stinkier I might add."

"You guys pulled the old "flaming crap" gag didn't you?" he said, laughing so loud I'm sure he could be heard in China.

"How sweet it was too. Watching that crap fly through the air, landing perfectly to give her highness a royal snack, was better than landing a double back." Naughty me, I couldn't begin to wipe the smile off my face.

"No way, was it Mark and the twins?" he asked, already knowing the answer.

"I'm not one to rat out my friends or enemies. Give me a break, will ya?" I replied in my most proper tone, adding a wink at the end even though I knew he couldn't see it.

"Man, this is one time I'm really glad I live next to that wench. I wouldn't have wanted to miss that for a naked picture of Fergie. Okay, that might be pushing it, but you should have invited me along. I would have donated my most fabulous body to science to have had my name on that one with you guys."

"I didn't even know we were going to do that." With that I spilled out the whole awful story about the doll on the noose. He completely understood why my brother reacted the way he did. We talked for a little bit longer and then hung up. I was too wound up to sleep, but I went to my room to hang out anyway…like usual. It was my one safe harbor. I loved it in there.

Sitting on my bed with my legs crossed, the vision of the doll popped into my head again, and I felt a chill go through me. I hate horror movies, especially the ones with little kids, and that reminded me of a little kid in a horror movie. Creepy.

Lying back onto my huge mound of pillows and stuffed animals, I grabbed Charlie from the top of the pile where he was reserved a special spot and gave him a squeeze. Charlie is the one I tell all my secrets to. I know he'll never judge me. He's the best listener, never interrupts, and always wipes my tears if I need him to. This blessed little neon patchwork stuffed turtle was a Valentine's Day gift from my parents when I was five. He was my favorite turtle in the whole wide world, and nothing was more comforting when I needed it than his huge, florescent, orange-and-pink shell. Charlie keeps me safe. I snuggled in with my buddy, and before I knew it, I was fast asleep.

CHAPTER TEN

"Get away from me!" I screamed as the man and his crew of chanting witches approached me. When they were close enough to touch me, the man ordered one of the women to remove my dress and cover my eyes. She obeyed her master and reached for the bottom of my makeshift dress.

"Leave me alone! Leave me alone!" I cried, flailing wildly against my shackled wrists and ankles. As the woman neared my face, I launched my face toward hers with the hope of catching some of her skin between my teeth. I caught her wrist in my mouth instead and held, biting down with every ounce of strength I could find. A coppery taste filled my mouth, and I knew I'd drawn blood. Gratification swept over me as she screeched and jerked her hand back, letting my dress fell back to my knees.

The man was furious, but instead of screaming, he released the most sinister laugh I had ever heard in my life. At that moment, I knew he had expected that exact reaction from me, but he was using his witch to wear me down so I wouldn't have any energy left to fight him. As he approached me, he ordered all the women to leave the barn. The look in his eyes was pure evil, and I could feel my legs go weak as all the blood rushed out of them and straight to my thumping heart. The world closed in around me, and fear sent me into unconsciousness.

I don't know how long I was out, but when I opened my eyes, the man had pulled my dress up and tucked it in around my neck. It was so tight that I had trouble breathing. *Try to relax and breathe through your nose,* I told myself in my mind. I knew that if I let myself panic, the air would be gone—constricted so much that I would not be able to get it down through my throat and into my lungs where it was desperately needed. Concentrating on breathing helped me block out what the man was doing to the most private parts of my body.

He was shoving something inside of me. What was it? My mind was screaming. I couldn't see. *Oh my God, it hurts so badly. Take it out! Take it out!* I could hear my cries for help in my head, but I couldn't make the words come out. I was too afraid to speak, knowing it would anger the master and make him hurt me even more. Silently in my head, I concentrated on making the air in my lungs go in and out in big waves and prayed for the pain to stop.

"Sam!" my mom said, shaking me out of my dream. "What are you dreaming about? You're making the strangest face."

Shaking my head like a paint mixer to clear not only my eyes but my head as well, I groggily mumbled, "Gee, Mom, dreams are so dumb. They seem so real and then you can't remember one single detail." Lying to my mom wasn't a favorite past time of mine, but this was one of those need-to-know moments, and frankly, she didn't need to know.

"Come on, sleepy head, time to get moving," she said as she gave me one last tickle on my shoulder with her long, cotton-candy-colored fingernails. "By the way, there's something on your ear."

As soon as she slipped out the door, my hand instinctively went to the left side of my head. My fingers wandered every millimeter of the fuzzy surface and stopped suddenly on a crusty substance located right behind my lobe. For a few seconds, I picked at the nastiness until it felt like I had removed all of it from my body. Sick as it was, I smelled my hand and almost gagged. It was cow poop.

Oh my God, if my mom realized what was on me, she would inevitably know exactly where it came from. I had to find Mark and warn him. *This could be bad,* I thought as I leapt out of my bed and ran full speed toward my brother's room.

"Mark!" I whispered with more volume than I had planned, unsuccessfully hiding the panic that was in my voice. "Get up, we got trouble, dude!"

Pulling his pillow over his head, he groaned as he lazily attempted to flop over on his side, "Mouse, get out…I have three and a half more minutes before my alarm goes off."

I gave his pillow a giant whack and told him about mom finding the poop on my neck. Instantly he sat up half laughing, half pissed and whispered back, "You dork. How'd you get that on you?"

"I don't know. Maybe I got a little on my hand and scratched my ear when you guys showed it to me…and I'm not a dork. You're the dork. Don't forget, you're the bulb with the bright idea to burn cow poop on the doorstep of a neighbor. Duh." I rolled my eyes and sighed. "Now who's the dork?" I added as I stomped out of his room more angry at being called a dork than the fact that he couldn't have reacted any stupider if he was actually trying. *Wait a minute, is* stupider *even a word? Oh well,* I thought to myself, *who cares? It fits him. Plus I didn't say it out loud.*

CHAPTER ELEVEN

Arriving at school that morning, it only took a few steps in the door before I noticed a buzz in the air. Curiosity left my face looking like I recently had it slammed and stuck in a bus door. When Amanda saw me I must have still had a scrunchy face because she stopped right in front of me, bent over to get right in my face, and molded her own mug into a mirror image of my own.

"What's up with your face, my little friend? You don't look much like a mouse today, more like a baby bulldog."

"It feels funny in here," I answered, trying to iron out the wrinkles I obviously had in my face.

"Funny, how?" she asked.

"Like something's going on or happened or something. Can't you feel it? It's totally buggin' me out. I mean, look around, nobody's walking the halls. They're all piled up like a herd of cattle when it's going to storm outside."

I took a breath and looked around then said more to myself than her, "Weird." Looking Mandy in the eyes I whispered, "Wanna come and eavesdrop on one of the smaller piles of people?" Once again I scanned the crowds. "Hey, there's JoAnna. It's impossible for her to talk at less than twelve decibels. Let's go stand close to her. She always seems to have a way of knowing the scoop."

"Okay, but we have to be incognito," Amanda whispered as she casually scanned the area. "We don't want anyone knowing we're listening in on their conversation. That could actually cause more damage to your face than was there a minute ago."

I gave her my best mad face and grabbed her by the arm, and together we ducked our heads and engaged our stealth tactics to get close to the one girl in our school who talked like there was permanently a B-1 bomber flying over head. We must have been sending out some pretty funky ESP waves because we hadn't been in our covert hiding place more than a couple of seconds when suddenly three other girls appeared out of nowhere, conveniently joining up with the two of us.

Together the five of us tried to carry on a fake conversation, all the while listening in on the voices coming from the circle directly to our right.

"I can't believe he did that," I heard JoAnna tell her friends.

"Me either," added her best friend, Marie.

Another girl in their circle continued, "Who were the three girls?"

Pulling my attention back to my own little group just for a quick question I asked, "Who are they talking about? What the heck happened?" Nobody answered any of my questions. We all just focused our attention on the intense conversation beside us.

"I heard they were only third graders." One of the girls said, shutting her eyes, trying to stop the tears that were about to stream down her cheeks.

In a consoling voice, JoAnna said, "I'm not sure, but I do know that Mrs. Bitner is not teaching her second graders today. I would be too if my husband was arrested for feeling up little girls. That's totally sick and wrong. If anyone ever did that to me or my sister, my dad would have hunted him down and shot him in the face with his biggest shotgun."

In a voice only Amanda could hear, I asked, "I don't get it. What is 'feeling up'?"

Without taking her eyes off JoAnna, she quietly answered, "Touching their privates, dummy." Then turning her head to look at me, she added, "You seriously didn't know that? Do you live under a rock?"

Hearing Mandy's words sent a massive rush of blood through my entire body, making me numb all over. She noticed something was wrong even before I did. The words had barely left her mouth when I felt her long, slim, muscular arm catching me around the waist a split second before I completely lost all feeling in my legs and crumbled to the floor.

As if it were planned, Mandy shuffled me toward the girls' bathroom right across the hall from where we were standing. Neither of us spoke a word as we maneuvered through the massive crowd that had recently gathered in that area of the hall. As soon as we pushed our way through the bathroom doors, Mandy let go of my waist and carefully propped my Jell-O-like body up against the wall under the row of mirrors. When she thought I was securely balanced, she cautiously investigated each and every stall, making sure no one else was there. I was in such a trancelike state that I didn't even notice that, just like a snail on the inside of a beautiful aquarium feeding on the bacteria growing on the clear glass walls, I languidly crept down the wall, creating a puddle of pure nothingness on the dirty, pink-and-white tiled floor. Just as I hit, I felt the world closing in around me as if I were floating down a familiar, dark, silvery tunnel. By the time she returned, I was curled up in a ball, sweaty and out cold.

"No!" I screamed as I felt an icy-wet sensation on my face. "Get away!" I yelled, pushing myself up to a sitting position and trying desperately to focus my eyes on my surroundings.

"Calm down, Sam," Mandy said sweetly as she once again pressed the cold, wet paper towel to my forehead. "It's okay. I'm here."

"What are you doing?" I asked as soon as Amanda's face came to focus. I looked around confused, "Why are we in here?"

"It was weird, as soon as you understood what Mr. Bitner did to those girls, you darn near fainted right there in the hall in front of everyone," she told me. "I shuffled you in here before you actually went out. What brought that on?"

Her words came flooding back, and I whispered more to myself than to her, "Oh my God, now I remember." With tears welling up in my eyes, just hanging on the edge of my bottom lid, I asked my trusted friend, "Mandy?" I sighed and rubbed the tears away, hoping she hadn't noticed, "Is he really going to jail?"

The look on her face told me everything I needed to know. It was not only invasive what he'd done to the girls, but it was illegal as well. Flopping over and pushing her weight toward me butt first, coming so close she was nearly sitting in my lap, she put her hand on mine. "Yes, I believe he is…for a long time."

"Do they all go to jail?" I asked as the tears finally slipped down my cheeks.

Gently she asked, "Sam, does this have anything to do with that cousin who stayed with your grandma and grandpa after his parents died in that fire?" I didn't answer. I couldn't. Every word that I wanted to come out froze solid in my throat.

For what seemed like forever but was probably only a few minutes, we just sat, tears slowly making their way down my cheeks, and when I finally looked up, she had tracks on her face too.

I flipped my hand palm up so the inside of my hand was against the inside of hers, and as I gave it a little squeeze, I dropped my head to my chest. "Please don't ever tell anyone," I begged. "They already think I'm a freak. In my wildest dreams I can't imagine what Becky would do if she even had any idea." After a long pause, I added in almost a whisper, "…and he warned me that I'd meet the same fate as his parents if I ever…" I let the words trail off into silence as fear captured my voice.

Turning to face me and gathering up my other hand into hers as well, she pulled our joined hands to her chest and said through her quiet cries, "Mouse, I am here for you. You never have to worry about me saying anything to anyone." A few seconds later, she put her right index finger under my chin, lifted my face, and whispered caringly, "How many times?"

Without any control of my mouth, I started talking. I'm not even sure what I said, but when I went quiet, Mandy uttered, "You have to talk to someone about this. What can I do?"

Sheer panic swept through me as she spoke those last words and just above a whisper I said, "No, nobody can ever know! He's gone now, and it's done! You have to promise you won't tell anyone ever!" I put my face in my hands and sobbed. "Please, Mandy, please, you have to swear not to ever say a word."

Through a sigh, she asked, "Have they ever found out where he disappeared to?" When I didn't answer her question, she once again she pulled my hands away from my face. Looking me straight in the eye, she repeated her promise to never tell. From the hall, we could hear the two-minute bell ring, and both of us slowly made our way up from the floor.

Before we left the girls' room, Mandy grabbed me strongly and hugged me so hard I thought I was going pass out again. "Hey, girl, lighten up a little. You're squishing me," I said, forcing a smile. Smiling back at me, she gave me another quick squeeze. Just in time to make a scene, guess who swooped in on her broom, Becky Miles.

"Whoa, what do we have here?" She smirked as she stood in the open doorway. Not wasting a second, she grabbed the door just as it was about to close and yelled out to her coven, "Hey, ladies, looks like we have a couple of lesbos on our hands! Check this out!"

Turning back to look at us, she mocked, "This town is totally going to crap. First a pervert and now lesbians."

Disgusted and not afraid at all, Mandy grabbed my hand and pulled me toward the door. Giving Becky a shove to make room for the two of us to get out, Mandy sneered and said, "Becky, why don't you go French kiss the math teacher? Then maybe you'll at least pass one class." And with that, we barged right past her royal highness.

As soon as we got around the corner and out of Becky's line of sight, Mandy looked at me at asked, "What do ya think, Mouse? Pretty good one, huh?" By the look on my face, Mandy could tell that I had no idea what on this earth she was talking about.

"Sam, you don't know what French kissing is either, do you?" she gently asked.

Letting out a big sigh, I answered her question with one of my own, "How do you?"

She let out a laugh, leaned closer to me and said, "Dope, I have four older brothers and a couple of parents who are of the firm belief that the more they explain about sex, the less my brothers are likely to try."

"Gross, French kissing is sex…and your parents tell you how to do it? Girlfriend, that's nasty."

Laughing out loud, Amanda added, "No dummy, French kissing isn't sex, it's when you're kissing someone and you put your tongues in each other's mouths."

"Okay, you're not allowed to talk anymore today. That's disgusting. Just think of all the germs. Ewww!" I said with a major grimace on my face.

"Oh, my little friend, we do need to talk," Mandy said as she threw one arm over my shoulder, letting her hand dangle precariously close to my ever-so-tender marble boob and continued bobbing her head as she spoke, "Girl, doesn't anyone tell you anything?"

Returning her head bobble and giving a little attitude to boot, I said, "My parents would chop off all their fingers and then drink battery acid before they'd ever talk about sex with my brother or me."

As we approached our classroom, Mandy added, "Sam, I got to hand it to ya, you are one tough cookie to keep your secret so long. And remember, a promise is a promise."

Inside my heart I knew that she meant what she said; however, my stomach wasn't quite so trusting. Not one minute of the day went by that I wasn't thinking about what had happened in the bathroom, and I was kicking myself for being such a baby and blabbing like a total freak. Every time the bell marking the end of a class rang, I bolted to the bathroom to throw up. My tummy was in knots just thinking about what I'd actually blurted to Mandy that morning. *I am such a stupid jerk!*

Finally, three thirty came, and hearing that last bell of the day was the answer to the bazillion prayers I'd said since hearing about what Mr. Bitner did to those girls. Invisibly blending into the drab, off-white paint on the wall, I hightailed it for my locker so I could get out of that place and run until my legs fell off. I needed air, now.

CHAPTER TWELVE

As I burst through the front door trying to wipe the waterfall of sweat out of my burning eyes, my mother stood on the steps glaring at me. I know that look, and I knew what was coming. Just as that thought went through my head, my mom screamed, "Samantha Anne Nelson! Where have you been? School has been out for hours and so has track practice! I've been worried sick. Do you realize your dad and your brother are out driving around the countryside trying to find you? Don't you know how to use a phone anymore? This is ridiculous, young lady. What have you got to say for yourself?"

Then as she stepped closer to me, her face transformed, and she said, "You're soaked. Why are you all wet? Are you hurt?"

Her questions came flying at me so fast that it took me a minute to sort through them, think of a somewhat believable answer, and find my voice, which at the time was buried so deep in the lump that had built up in my throat all day I wasn't sure anything was going to come out of my mouth even if I tried to speak. Instead, for some crazy reason, tears began flooding my eyes, creating a tsunami down my face, but no words would come.

When the fact that I was actually crying and unable to speak registered in my mom's head, she stopped yelling at me and quietly asked, "What happened, Sam?"

Remembering some show I'd watched about meditation and yoga, I tried to calm myself by sucking in a couple of super deep breaths. Shocked that it actually worked, I stared at the floor, wiping my tears and snot on the bottom of my already soaked T-shirt, and uttered through quiet gasps, "It was a mega-bad day. I was just out running off steam."

"Were the girls at you again today?" she asked with concern, touching my shoulder to guide me to my room.

"You could say that," I answered. Slowly I turned my head to her and a moment later asked, "Is it true what everyone is saying about Mr. Bitner?"

She didn't answer my question until we were safely in my room. Then she simply said, "That's what people are saying." She sat down on my bed as I plopped down on the floor to stretch. Adamantly she added, "But I won't believe it until it's actually proven. Some people will make up anything to get attention. You of all people should know that with the way Becky has lied through her teeth all these years just to get you in trouble."

"I know, Mom, but how did those little girls know that what he did was wrong, and they should tell?" I whispered in response, leaning over to grab my feet.

Watching me, she diverted from the subject, "People aren't meant to bend like that dear. Yikes." She groaned, "Ohhh, don't hurt yourself."

I peeked up at her, smiled, and said, "I have no idea what you're talking about."

She continued, "What I heard uptown today was that one of their moms overheard them talking about it at a sleepover, and she immediately called their family pastor to see what she should do. You'd think with all his training in family counseling that he'd have gone right over there to talk to them. His response was so confusing to me. I can't believe he would have her call the police before he actually had a heart-to-heart with those girls. I mean, come on. They're only little girls. It had to be the most terrifying night for everyone involved." She paused and looked down at the floor for a second. Then without even looking up, she shook her head and added, "I can't even imagine what your father and I would do to someone if they hurt you like that."

Her last comment instantly made my seriously empty stomach think it was on a tilt-a-whirl causing all the acid to shoot up my esophagus and come dangerously close to spewing out my mouth. Swallowing the bile, I asked, "Mom, can I go take a shower now and just go to bed? This has been a totally crappy day."

"After all those miles I'm sure you put on, you need to eat something. Dinner is in the fridge, just nuke it first or it probably won't taste very good," she encouraged.

"I don't think I can eat right now. I'm too tired," I said as I got up and started toward my room.

"Hey, when was the last time you ate? You need to eat or you're going to be sick," she said as she followed me to my room. Gently touching my shoulder to turn me around to face her, she asked, "Sam, when was the last time you've eaten anything? All I ever see you do is chew gum and work out."

Dodging her questions, I turned away so as to not have to look her in the eye when I blatantly fibbed as I answered, "I ate lunch at school today."

"Okay, honey." She gasped as she left my room. As I was following her out the door, she quickly did an about-face, running right into me, knocking me to my butt, and added through a little giggle, "Sorry. Get some rest. But you do need to eat more. A light breeze could blow you away right now." She said as she gave me a hand up off the floor. As she walked away, I couldn't kick my verbal filter in quick enough to catch my next dumb comment, "…or a big mama."

Turning to head to the shower under my breath and rolling my eyes, I added, "Whatever…so skinny I'll be too gross to mess with, or even better, I'll starve to death. Either way, who cares? Nobody around here ever notices anything that matters anyway." With that I took a shower and headed straight for my room to finish what little homework I had and sleep everything away.

In less than an hour I was done writing my essay for history, but I wasn't tired. The conversation Mandy and I had in the bathroom kept digging into my memory like a mole trying to get to China. The urge to talk to my friend took over, and I slipped out of bed in search of my shoes.

Thankfully my bedroom window sat just above the ground, making sneaking out a breeze. This being my first time, I took extra care not to make a sound. I wound the window open and silently crawled out onto the yard. When I looked back toward our house, I could see my mom's reading light on and knew it would only be a matter of minutes before they were both out cold. Relieved they hadn't heard my escape, I turned and started running in the direction of Mandy's house.

CHAPTER THIRTEEN

Ten minutes later, I found myself outside the sliding glass door that led into Mandy's frilly pink bedroom. Silently I listened for any sign that she might be awake. From the other side of the window, I heard a phone ringing, and then Mandy said, "Is this the right thing to be doing?"

No one answered her question and the ringing continued in the background. Then the ringing suddenly stopped and a man's voice came from somewhere in her room. "Hello?" he said sleepily.

I leaned closer to the glass door. Her curtains were slightly open in the center, and I could see her pacing around the room. She was alone from what I could tell, but she answered the man's voice as if talking on the phone. Then it hit me. She had her phone on speaker. I crouched down and put my ear close to the glass.

Her voice sounded nervous as Mandy said, "Hello, is Dani home?"

"Dani, what the heck is she calling Dani for?" I wondered out loud to myself. Hearing my voice, I quickly clasped my hands over my mouth and continued to listen.

"No, she's out right now. This is her dad," the raspy voice on the other end said. "Can I give her a message?" Stifling his smoker's cough, he continued. "I expect her and her ma to be back from the city any time now," he said a bit more awake.

"Could you please have her call Mandy? I'm a friend of Sami's, and I really need to talk to her about something important."

"Sure." He paused slightly before adding, "Everything all right with my little Mouse? She didn't break her neck doing one of those flipping things she does, did she?" he added, unable to hide the fatherly concern from his voice. Then without warning, he went in a different direction all together. "Hey, did she ever tell you I'm the one gave her that nickname?" From my point of view I could see Mandy grin, and I couldn't help for smile myself. His redneck drawl continued. "Yep, fits that little twerp perfectly if I do say so myself." Gurgly chuckling came through the phone speaker, and I saw Mandy grimace toward her phone at the nasty sound.

As soon as she thought he might be able to hear her once again, Mandy added, "No, sir, she didn't tell me that, and no she's not hurt either. Besides, it's track season. She just told me a totally major huge secret, and I think Dani should know about," she shot back quickly, attempting to make it a nice, short, and sweet conversation with Mr. Roy Ivans.

After she heard a sigh of relief coming from his end of the phone, he chuckled, "You girls is a funny bunch. A secret, huh? Well, okay then, what's yer number?" Hearing the sound of a drawer being ransacked on the other end of the line, Mandy figured he didn't have a pen ready. As fast as that thought entered and exited her mind, he added, "Whoa, hang on a sec while I grab something to write with. I'm guessing a pen might come in handy for writin,' and since my mind ain't what it was when I was in my thirties, I'd better not rely on my old brain with somethin' this important." As he searched for a pen, his whiskers made a scratching noise against the receiver. About thirty seconds later, he came back, "Okay, little girl, shoot."

"This is Mandy from her old school, and she can reach me at 236-555-0889, no matter how late it is, 'kay?"

"That was Mandy at 236-555-0889?"

"Yes, sir, perfect."

"Hey, I'm just an old farmer at heart. No need to be calling me sir. Roy is good enough, Miss Mandy. I'll make sure to give her yer message, but she just had her seventh round of chemo and might not be her chipper self. Actually, she might have to call you between trips to the bathroom. They've really been tearing up her stomach these past few times."

"Thanks a lot, Roy," Mandy said before quickly hanging up the phone.

Standing in the middle of her room, she was smiling at the odd conversation she'd just had with Dani's dad cell phone still in hand.

Standing, I reached out to knock on her door. From the other side, I could hear her phone ring. Quickly I yanked my hand back from the glass and dropped back to my hiding spot to listen. Through the peephole in the curtains I watched as she walked toward me. My stomach started to swirl. I didn't want her to think I was spying on her, even though I actually was. I wiggled sideways to get out from in front of her door and heard her say, "Hello?" as she pulled open the glass part of the door, leaving the screen shut to the outside. This made listening much more convenient, and I could hear the entire conversation from where I hid.

"Oh, thank God you're still there. What's wrong with Samantha? Is she okay? What kind of secret do you know? Come on, woman. Answer me. I'm dying here!" Dani spat in a frenzied female voice through the speaker. *Yes,* I thought as I relaxed into my spot next to the house. *Mandy has put this conversation on speakerphone as well.* Quietly, I listened as my two friends discussed what had taken place that day.

"Dani?" Mandy asked, trying to slow down the pace a little. "Is this you?"

"Of course it's me. Who else would it be? What's up with Sam?" she said, dropping the speed of her words down to two hundred a minute.

"First, you need to slow down a bit. Relax. Physically she's fine. No problem there. She's healthy as a horse and pretty sure she could actually pull a plow…or two." Mandy said reassuringly. I couldn't help but grin at that one.

"Physically? Why did you say it like that? I hear a "but" coming," she added suspiciously. "Come on, Mandy, spill it."

"Wait, let me start at the beginning so this makes sense. There's been a rumor going around about some trouble that Mrs. Bitner's husband has gotten himself into," she began.

"Mrs. Bitner? Like as in our second grade teacher, Mrs. Bitner?" Dani questioned.

"That's exactly the one," answered Mandy.

"What kind of rumor about him could be going around? From what I remember, he's just a crabby, old, retired fart."

With a sigh, Mandy added, "More like a crabby, old, retired fart with wood for little kids."

"No way! You're kidding, right?" She couldn't hide the urgency that was slipping out in her voice. "Did he do something rotten to Samamtha? 'Cause if he did, I'm coming there and shooting him myself!" Dani yelled into the phone, "right in the nuts."

"Calm down. No, *he* didn't hurt Sami," Amanda said hesitantly into the phone making sure to emphasize the *he*.

"I don't like the way you said *he*. What's really going on?" This time Dani's voice was quiet when she spoke.

Mandy could hear the impatience beginning to ebb in her voice and thought it best to just get it over with. "Okay, but I promised her I would not tell another living soul, so you have to promise never to repeat what I'm going to tell you ever in your life."

"Okay, okay, I probably won't be around much longer for you to worry about me telling anyway," she said, obviously frustrated now.

Mandy caught her dig on herself, but she let her comment go in one ear and out the other and just decided to go straight in on what she had to say. "Today at school, we overheard some kids talking about Mr. Bitner getting arrested for molesting three little girls, so we sneaked around until we found JoAnna. You remember her—Miss Blabber Mouth of the Century?"

"Yeah, I remember her. She couldn't keep her mouth shut about anything she overheard her mom and dad talking about. Is her mom still the secretary to that lawyer or whatever?" From my hiding spot, I gave my friend a silent fist pump of approval.

"Yes ma'am, and her office has a bird's-eye view of where they bring in people who were just arrested. JoAnna said her mom actually typed up the report telling what he did and to whom. Now she's spreading it all over the school."

"Who did he hurt?" Dani asked.

Inhaling deeply Mandy answered, "That I don't know, but I do know that it wasn't Sami."

"Then what does this have to do with her?"

"Well, after we heard JoAnna tell her friends what he'd been arrested for, Sami didn't get it until I explained what 'felt up' meant."

With a chuckle similar to her father Dani said, "That's my Mouse, naive to the nth degree." I stuck my tongue out in the direction of my friends.

"It's not funny. As soon as she realized what had really happened to those girls, she turned pure white, and I thought she was going to pass out right in the hall. So I grabbed her and drug her into the bathroom just in time," Mandy spat into the phone.

"What did you do? What did she tell you? Dani demanded, forgetting all about the entertaining naivety of her friend.

"Do you remember that kid who moved in with her grandma and grandpa because his parents died in a fire? Sami's creepy cousin." Mandy went on. At the mention of him, a knot closed my throat, and I had to swallow hard to keep from giving myself away.

"Yeah, he was creepy. I always thought he was a great combination of a skater version of Ted Bundy." There was a long pause. Then she added, "Hey, didn't he burn his parents to death?" Dani asked quietly into the phone.

"That's the one, Monte something or other. Turns out, he did horrible things to Sami too before he disappeared into thin air," Mandy whispered back, not actually knowing why they were both whispering at the moment.

Her voice on the edge of cracking, Dani asked, "What do you mean by"—she gulped loudly—"horrible?" Fear caused every muscle in my body to tense. "Please, don't tell, please don't tell," I whispered to myself.

"Sami really didn't tell me any details, only that he was always touching her where he shouldn't and making her do things by threatening to kill her if she didn't do exactly what he told her to." Thankful for her discretion, I relaxed and kept listening.

I could tell Dani was crying when she gasped, "Oh my God, Mandy, horrible doesn't even come close. She never told me. I can't begin to imagine the fear she's lived in after what he did to her. It certainly explains a ton about why she is the way she is, doesn't it?

"That's the understatement of the year. We have to help her. What do you think I should do? I'm scared, D." My friend was silent, and I was touched by her concern.

"Me too," she said, and for several seconds no one said a word. We all just sat in mutual thought.

With a huge sigh, Dani finally said, "Mandy, you still go to the same church as Sam?"

"Yeah, why?" she asked.

"We need an adult for this one. See if you can go talk to Pastor Paul. From what I remember, he's pretty awesome and will hopefully know what to do."

"Okay, right after school tomorrow I'll run over to the church. Sam is going shopping with her mom after track in Madison for the weekend, so she won't even be in town. That will work out great. I'll call you right after I talk to him," Mandy promised.

"Perfect. But hey, if you can, call me when you're with him so I can listen to what he says too, 'kay?"

"No prob. Talk to you tomorrow. Bye," Amanda said as I saw her reach to push the off button. Just before she got her finger there, she heard Dani close up the conversation.

"Tomorrow then…bye. Hey! Mandy!" she yelled into the receiver. I stiffened in my spot.

Quickly yanking her hand back, Mandy said, "Yeah?"

"Thanks. I'm glad she has you there with her," she said, her voice cracking once again. My heart melted, and I felt warm wet tears begin to trickle down my cheeks.

"Me too. Talk to you tomorrow," she uttered sadly, and this time hung up the phone.

Feeling warm at the thought of the protectiveness my two friends had just shown me, I wiped my face with the back of my hand and stood up. Slowly I walked back home, tossing the conversation I'd just overheard around in my mind. I was so relieved that Mandy hadn't given Dani any details of what I'd told her. Come to think of it, what had I all told her? My nerves were suddenly on edge once again, and anxiety took over. I'd never be able to sleep now. Maybe a hot shower would help.

CHAPTER FOURTEEN

Standing in the shower, letting the steaming hot water wash away all the sweat and tears from my horrific day away, I tried to get my mind to concentrate on anything but the undoubtedly haunting dreams that were to come when sleep finally captured me for the day. My battle with trying to remember what I'd told Mandy lasted at least a half an hour, when a knock on the bathroom door broke me free from my reverie, and I remembered that I was still in the shower. "Sami, honey, you've been in there a long time. Are you all right?" my mom called from behind the door.

Thinking fast on my shriveled-up feet, I yelled back once again, consciously lying to my mother, "Yes, Mom, I just finished shaving my legs. Be out in a sec."

"Okay, just checking. I thought maybe a giant sewer snake had eaten you up for dinner."

With the best fake chuckle I could muster, I replied, "Nope, he wouldn't want me for dinner, but I might make a good midnight snack."

Listening intently, I quietly dried my legs off before stepping out of the shower and breathed a sigh of relief as I heard her walking away, laughing to herself. I finished drying off, slung one of the white work T-shirts I nabbed from my dad's underwear drawer over my head, and pulled it down over my still wet butt as I left the bathroom and rounded the corner to my room. After flicking on the twenty-six-inch TV hanging on my wall, I reached mindlessly for the worn deck of cards that sat on my night stand, jumped into bed, and folded my legs what we called "Indian style" and went to work. I was antsy and needed to keep busy, so the TV provided the noise my mind desired, and the cards kept my physical being busy so as to not fall asleep too quickly. I was pro at solitaire. My dad would watch me play on the living room floor sometimes and tell me I must have been a dealer in Vegas in a past life. I have to admit, playing several hundred hands of solitaire a week did make me pretty much totally super-duper fast at shuffling and dealing cards.

After about an hour of winning and losing, I could feel my eyes getting heavy and my head bobbing. Unconsciously, I gave up the fight and surrendered not only to my pillow but to sleep itself. As I sunk deeper and deeper into the abyss, I felt something warm on my feet.

"Stop!" I screamed. "Please, Mister, these are my new shoes Mommy just bought me today!" I cried out as the man held me precariously over a cauldron of steaming liquid that hung from thick chains bolted into one of the timbers in the rafters of the barn, directly over a blazing fire. "No, no, no! No water. Hot! Hot! Hot!"

He wouldn't listen. As I felt the squeeze of his hands around my ribcage and heat penetrating the patent black leather of my Mary Janes, in a final, desperate scream, I wailed, tucking my legs tightly into a fetal position against my quivering frame. "I'll be a good girl, I'll be good, I promise."

He pulled my tiny face right up next to his and whispered between his teeth, "Put your feet down, you brat, or I'll cut them off." His breath was a putrid mixture of old cigarette smoke, coffee, and some other rancid, unfamiliar smell. He inhaled deeply, blew another grotesque breath into my nostrils, inhaled again, and spoke, "You're dirty, and I want to play." He extended his arms and held me directly over the boiling water once again, "Now drop those skinny little legs, or I'll drop you from here." He smiled and relaxed his tone. "I have a surprise for you today." He inhaled again and in a sarcastically sweet tone added, "My little darling."

Trying desperately to hide my panic, I released my legs from my body, and the man lowered me into the boiling tub of water. As the heat reached my knees, my feet finally touched the bottom. I gave into the burning sensation and couldn't stop the tears from rolling down my cheeks. The master seemed to relish in the fact that he was hurting me, and he let an evil smile creep across his wrinkled, unshaven face at the sight. The thought of causing pain only excited him. His breath quickened as he slowly forced me to sit in the steaming water, staring intently into my eyes.

From somewhere in the barn, I heard a noise I recognized. "Thank you, God," I whispered to myself. I turned my head right and then left, in search of my rescuer's position. "No," I whispered again when I saw one of the master's women being dragged toward me by a dog the size of a horse. I'd never seen a dog like this in real life, only in a movie...*Beethoven.* "St. Bernard," I heard myself say as I leaned forward and grabbed the sides of the tub, staring at the beast coming toward me.

"Very good, my dear," the master said out loud. "Do you like your surprise? He's bigger than you and very dirty too—just like you."

My skin crawled, and the hair on the back of my neck stood straight up as I realized the drooling hairy beast was focused on me. "What...?" I started to ask and then thought better of it not wanting to give the master any ideas.

As if he could read my mind, the master answered my unspoken question, "Yes, my dear, the two of you are going to become very good friends." Changing his focus from the dog to me, he thrust his hands into the warmth and stripped me of my nightgown, purposely leaving my shoes on my feet. "Isn't he beautiful...all that hair?"

Before I could take in a breath, he slammed my head under the water and held it there until my lungs burned. Thrashing my limbs, I prayed for it to end. Just before my body was going to suck in water where air should be, the man pulled my head out of the water, let out a loud laugh, and as I gasped for breath, he submerged my head again. This time I felt a violent jolt as my body smashed into the bottom of the vat. The weight made it impossible for me to fight my adversary this time.

At the last second, the weight moved to the side, releasing my body, and the man dragged me to the surface by my hair. He dangled me firmly over the water for several seconds, allowing me to catch my breath.

He backed away from the tub, and I forced myself not to look at him, but this angered him. He shouted to a witch nearby, "Bring the girl to me. I want that pleasure."

"Witch!" the master shouted, startling both of us. "Move away from that child! I'll take care of her."

"Yes, sir," the woman answered, bowing without raising her head to look directly at him. She then hurriedly clasped the leash to the collar, gave it a tug, and ordered him to come. As the dog bounded to the floor and followed the woman, I cautiously peeked over the rim of the tub to see the master slowly removing his trousers. Quickly, I ducked my head back down behind the edge, clenching my eyes tightly shut. I sat perfectly still in my filthy prison, hoping he didn't see me. For several seconds, I heard nothing but dead silence. My curiosity got the best of me, and I slowly opened my eyes.

"Hello, my sweet," I heard from over the side of the tub. When I looked up, the Master was smiling down at me.

"I think it's time to play," he said as he reached in and slid his hands under my arms, lifting me out. The monster carried me straight out in front of his naked body all the while staring at me as he walked across the barn to an old, stained mattress that rested on the floor by the far wall. Setting me to my feet, he ordered, "Lay down."

"No," I defied him, walking backward away from him, not knowing the corner of the room was right behind me.

"Oh, I see, you want to play chase," he said, softly realizing I wasn't aware that I had no place to run. Smiling, moving closer to me, he said, "I like chase…makes the conquest ever more satisfying."

I stepped back once again and felt something touching each of my shoulders. I gasped and let out a little scream. He let out a chuckle and stepped right up in front of me. Thinking that if I threw myself backward I could knock the woman over and get away, I thrust myself backward as hard as I could. "Owww!" I screamed as a nail plunged deep into my left shoulder. It wasn't a woman behind me at all; he had launched my entire body weight into the corner of the room. The Master stepped up and reached his hands out toward me. "Come here, little one. You've hurt yourself."

"Get away from me, you freak!" I screamed. Ignoring the pain, I yanked my shoulder off the nail, ducked under his outstretched arms, and ran has hard as I could toward the only sunlight coming into the room. I was desperately hoping it was a door or a window.

"Ha, ha, ha," I could hear from behind me. "You are a fiery one. I like it…makes things interesting, but I will have you, child," the man continued as he walked heavily toward me.

I was trying not to listen to him and focused only on my exit. I knew if I let him in my head, he'd have that advantage too. Pumping my arms and legs with all my might, I finally reached the spot where light entered the darkness. It was a window. However, the window was at least fifteen feet up the wall. I searched in vain for a way up, and without warning, I felt myself flying through the air. Hitting the floor hard, I felt the weight of the man on top of me. He flipped me over to my back and held my hands up over my head tightly to the ground. He panted, "Game over. I win." Smiling down at me, he yelled, "Woman, get your sisters and secure this wild child in my chambers. I'm sick of foreplay!" Then he looked down at me. "Well, maybe in a minute," he said down to me quietly.

When the women came, the man continued to hold my arms down until a witch took his place. Then when another had my an-

ANGELA K. BENNETT

kles tightly in her grip, he scooted his body off to the side. A third
witch spread a large gray blanket on the floor next to me. When she
was finished, the others rolled me onto it, never letting their grip on
me loosen. They had me mummified so swiftly it was obvious they
had done this several times before. Working together, they hoisted
me into the air and carried me to where they were ordered.

"Keep the child secure while I prepare the shackles," I heard one
woman order the others.

"Yes, ma'am," both women answered in unison.

For several seconds, I hung in my cocoon, waiting for what was
to come next. Finally, the woman in charge ordered, "Secure the
child for Master." With that I felt my stomach come into contact
with a firm surface. Something cold was placed around each wrist
and ankle. Before the women attached the metal to the four corners
of the bed, they flipped me over to my back. As they began to pull
my limbs apart, I squeezed my eyes shut and let out a blood-curdling
scream, "Mom!"

"Sam, Sam, Sam!" I heard my mother's voice growing in volume
somewhere in the distance and opened my eyes just as she came
rushing through my bedroom door. "What is it, honey?" she said in
a panic. "Are you hurt? What is it?" She questioned quickly as she
ran over and sat on the side of my bed. I sat up and threw my arms
around her neck and started to cry. "What is it, Samantha? Talk.
You're scaring me," she begged.

"I can't feel my legs," I said, realizing it wasn't as big of a lie as
it sounded like.

"Wh—," she started to ask as she looked down at my folded
legs. "You goof, you fell asleep with your legs Indian style. No wonder." She chuckled and shoved me back down on the bed. "What
on earth were you thinking?" she said, reaching down to help me
straighten out my legs.

"Ohhhh," I moaned. "That's gonna really hurt when they start
waking up." I grimaced as I tried to stretch as far as I could.

"Just don't try to stand up for awhile or you'll end up on your face." She laughed as she got up and started back for my door.

"What time is it, Mom?" I called to her as she left.

"It's only nine thirty. Don't fall back asleep until your legs wake up," she said, and I could hear her laugh as she started telling my dad what was going on.

"Don't worry, I won't," I said, knowing full well she couldn't hear me. "Don't worry about that at all," I repeated as I reached for my deck of cards and the remote to my TV. After that one, I didn't want to ever go to sleep again.

CHAPTER FIFTEEN

Finally, the last day of seventh grade was over, and as I ran home, I was giddy with excitement, for tomorrow Mark was chauffeuring me to the Minneapolis Gymnastics Academy in the Twin Cities. Running down the alley behind Becky's house, I actually shouted, "Catch you on the flip side!" Once I said it, I realized the "punny" side of my comment and laughed all the way to the end of the alley.

Nothing could bring me down right then. I was floating on a cloud. Then I saw it. Fear caused my legs to go numb, and I nearly collapsed before I could come to a complete stop. As I stood frozen like a statue, it came closer and closer until it was staring me right in the eye. The beast circled me cautiously several times before wiping its wet, snotty nose against my hand. My stomach heaved, and I wretched on the ground in front of me. As the dog focused on licking up my vomit, I seized my moment and sprinted toward the safety of my house as fast as my legs could carry me. From out of nowhere, I felt something grab my wrist firmly and pull me even harder, causing me to run even faster. It was Mark. I'd told him about my dog dream, and he knew my terror.

When we flew into the garage, he panted, "Sorry for coming up behind you like that, Mouse, but I saw that dog circling you and could feel your fear."

In a blast of air, the rest of his pack flew into the open garage door. "Whoa, dude, what was that all about?

"Duh, you guys know Sami's afraid of dogs. Didn't you see that shepherd checking her out?" Mark said protectively.

"So? It was just Duke. He's harmless," Joe smarted off.

Smacking his buddy in the back of the head Mark said, "You jerk, you know she's scared to death of dogs."

"Yeah," he moaned to Mark. He looked at me and added, "Sorry, Sami, you okay?

"I'm fine," I said as I walked past them heading for the door to inside. "No thanks to you," I continued as I gave him a quick, playful push.

Reaching for the doorknob, I asked, "You dorks hanging around for awhile? You know I'm leaving tomorrow for the summer."

"Sure, what's for dinner?" Seth shouted as I turned and took a step inside. Then he chuckled, "You're not cookin' are ya, Mouse? I'd like to live to see my senior year."

"Whatever." I sneered, pretending to be offended by his comment and shut the door behind me.

Once inside, I leaned back against the door and took in a deep breath. My legs were still a little wobbly from my run-in with death and then my unnatural sprint home. Letting my breath out, I slipped off my tennis shoes and smiled at how much my brother meant to me. I didn't know what I'd ever do without him. "Don't even think that," I scolded myself out loud as I stepped toward the stairs that lead to my room. "Think about what to pack," I said.

The next morning came, and Mark and I took off on our road trip to Minneapolis Gymnastics Academy in the Twin Cities. This was our first "parent-free" road trip, and I was seriously pumped. Two hours alone with my bro, his awesome tunes at full volume, the sunroof open, and three months without Becky and the witches. Yes!

As we were pulling out of the driveway, I saw something strange out of the corner of my eye. I wasn't sure what it was, but it felt like someone was watching us. All the way to the cities, that feeling followed me. I didn't know if it was real or my mind playing tricks on me, but every once in a while throughout that summer, I felt like I was being watched. Sometimes I'd even smell an all-too-familiar smell. Was it leftover from my dream or real…stale cigarette smoke and rancid coffee. Why?

PART TWO
HIGH SCHOOL

CHAPTER SIXTEEN

For the next couple of years, Becky and the girls put the majority of their attention into exploring all the fringe benefits that boys came with. It was a nice relief to not be the center of their ridicule for a while. It left me focused on gymnastics and school. However, it seemed that when one door tried to close, another found its way open. The feeling of being followed was gradually becoming more and more disturbing. By tenth grade, I was totally freaked out and hypersensitive to being followed. Mark and I talked about it periodically, but even he thought I was being paranoid most of the time.

One spring day of my tenth-grade year, Mandy, two other older girls from our distance team, Liz and Mel, and I were on our way back to town from a long run for track practice. The route we were assigned was one that took us past an old, abandoned farm that created an anxiety in me I'll never be able to put into words. It was way too much like the place from my nightmare.

As we drew near the house, one of the girls looked toward the old farm and said, "Hey, anyone dare to see if the old place is as creepy as they say?"

"No way," I shot back too quickly.

"What's up with that, Sam? You don't actually believe in ghosts, do ya?" the other girl taunted.

Feeling the exaggerated tension in my voice, Mandy slowed her pace to meet mine and quietly whispered so only I could here, "What's up, chickee? It'll be fun. Let's check it out. Can't hurt anything, right?"

Our two teammates had already cut through the grassy ditch and were heading for the old barn when I slowed to a walk. Grabbing my friend's arm, I nervously said, "Mandy, it's just a feeling. This place gives me the creeps."

"I know. Me too," she added, grabbing my hand and guiding me into the ditch toward the old buildings, "But we can't let them know. Dude, they're seniors. We have to go." With a sharp tug on my arm, she rolled her eyes, chuckled, and said, "Suck it up."

I gave in to her tug and followed, trying to be as casual as I could. As we approached the barn, I saw a dark shadow flash through my peripheral vision. I froze in my tracks, causing Mandy's grip on my arm to snap away. She stumbled at the quick release. "What the heck…?"

From my frozen state, I whispered, "Mandy, did you see that?"

Playing along, she leaned forward, looked side to side quickly, and whispered back, "What?" Her posture relaxed and stepped close to my face. With a pretty forceful forehead slap, she laughed, "Give me a break, Mouse."

I shook off her slap and reached up to feel the spot she made contact with. "Hey, that hurt."

Before I regained my senses, she had a hold of my arm and was pulling me toward the building. "Your brain is playing tricks on you. Chill out. It was probably just a cat."

"Come on, you guys!" Liz yelled as she was waving at us from the partially open doorway. "Hurry up before the rest of the team comes by. Let's scare the crap out of them." We all ran in through the small crack, heaved the big door closed, and bounded up the rickety stairs two at a time to the hayloft. I realized I was bringing up the rear when a sudden burst of fear shot through me, causing my legs to give one huge, final leap to the top and quickly turn around, only to catch a glimpse of something behind me.

"Ha!" I gasped loud enough for the rest to hear, for they all turned and stared at me.

"What?" Mel said, giving me a dirty look. "Don't be so jumpy. You scared the crap out of me."

Turning to look back down the stairs, I said quietly, "Sorry, I thought I saw something at the bottom of the stairs."

"Sam, sit down! You're white!" Mandy shouted as she rushed over to grab my arm.

Feeling her strong fingers wrap around my arm, the all too familiar silver world began to close in on me as I spoke. "I'mmm fiiiiine." My words trailed off as silver turned to black.

When I woke up, I could hear Liz panicking in the distance. "We have to wake her up! Can't you smell that?" she screamed. "Smoke!" I could hear footsteps rushing all around me…close, far, close again. "This place is on fire."

Suddenly, I felt as though I was floating and forced my eyes to open a bit. "What's going on?" I mumbled almost inaudibly. As my focus returned, I could see that Liz was carrying my feet, and Mel and Mandy each had an arm. I wiggled out of their grip and tried to stand on my own. "Let me down," I insisted. "I can walk."

Mandy was the last to release me when she was certain I had my balance back. "Sam, you fainted again, and we have to get out of here."

"What stinks?" I grimaced as I was following her down the stairs to the main entrance.

Looking back over her shoulder at me, she shouted, "Just come on already…*Move!*" She reached up, more aggressive than I'd ever seen her, and pulled me down the step. "Hurry up! This place is on fire! We have to get out of here, *now!*"

Stumbling behind her down the stairs, I felt a surge of adrenaline, which caused my legs to leap through the open door. The four of us ran for the ditch. Instinctively, I looked back at the smoky structure, and once again, I caught a glimpse of what looked like someone watching us from the upstairs window in the burning barn. Gasping, I asked the others, "There's someone in there!"

"What? Where?" Mel asked in rapid succession, searching the building windows with her eyes.

Pulling me further away from the building, Mandy added, "I don't see anything."

When I knew Liz and Mel couldn't hear me, I whispered, "Mandy, I recognized that face."

She looked at me with fear and concern, "What do you mean, Sam?"

"It was him," I breathed. "I think…" I looked her directly in the eye, "He's here."

"We have to get out of here!" Mandy shouted, jumping to her feet. "Come on!"

The four of us hightailed it back to school. In the distance, we could hear the wailing of sirens and knew exactly where they were headed. Once we got into the locker room, Mel said, "I'm going to go find Coach. She needs to know about this."

Liz stepped in front of her, blocking the door, "If you tell, we'll have a lot of explaining to do, like what we were doing in that barn in the first place." She backed away from the entrance, and sitting down on the bench added, "I don't know about you, but I'm not about to tell anyone anything. We'd be in big trouble for even going near that place."

Mel thought for a second and then sat down on the bench. "You're right, but first, between just us four, do we agree that we all saw the same thing?" She paused. "I mean, there was a face in that window…right?"

"Yeah," I added quietly from across the room.

Mandy took a deep breath then pleaded to me, "Sam, it's time to spill it." She looked right at me, and the other two lifted their eyes in my direction too.

"Spill what, Sam?" Mel asked. "Who's that guy?"

Liz moved across the room closer to me and took a seat on the bench a few feet from where I was, "Girl, if you know something, you really need to get it off your chest." She reached out, touching my hand. "We're all in this together…and that guy is dangerous. We have to tell someone."

Pulling my hand quickly away from her touch, I looked directly at Mandy and didn't need to say a word. She knew exactly what I was thinking.

"Sam, let us help," she pleaded. "You know what he's capable of." Reaching out to me again, she said quietly, "You have to trust us."

I leaned my back up against the locker beside mine and slowly slid down to a sitting position on the floor with my legs pulled tightly to my chest. Dropping my head into my folded arms resting on my knees, I silently breathed the words I had never wanted to say out loud, "I know. He has to be stopped." I drew in a big breath, let it out, and said, barely audible, "Someone go get Coach before I change my mind."

CHAPTER SEVENTEEN

When Coach arrived in the locker room, she looked around at the four of us, obviously confused, "What's going on girls?" she asked.

The four of us made eye contact, and Mel said, "Come on, ladies, let's give them some privacy."

As they all stood to leave, I cried, "No!" I looked at Coach, "Mandy has to stay."

Coach moved her eyes to my friend and asked, "Mandy, are you okay with that?"

Mandy stopped with her hand holding the door open. "Of course, if you're sure, Sam. But are you sure you won't be more comfortable alone with Coach?"

I thought about her words for a minute, and the room stayed silent. It was as if this heavy secret sucked all the sound out of the room. Then I said, "You're probably right." And I laid my head back down on my forearms, pretending I was invisible to the world.

Once the door bumped completely shut, Coach got up, silently took out her keys, and went over and locked the door from the inside. Then, without saying anything, she sat back down next to me and waited patiently for me to start talking.

The whole Mr. Bitner thing constantly invaded my thoughts, and I didn't want anyone saying the things about my family that were floating around about theirs.

Finally, I spoke, "Did you hear the sirens?"

"Yes," she answered quietly.

"They were fire engines…right?" I questioned, knowing that answer already.

"Yes," she repeated.

"We were there," I admitted.

"Where?" Coach prodded gently.

"At the old barn."

"Did you girls set that fire, Sam?" she asked.

"No, ma'am." I sighed. I took another breath, and when I let it out, I added, "He did."

"Who, Sam? Who are you talking about?" She continued to coax, half turning toward me.

"My cousin, Monte." I looked up at her. "You remember that kid whose parents died a few years ago and then moved in with my grandma and grandpa?"

"Your grandma's sister's kid, right?" She paused for an instant then added, "Didn't his parents die in a fire?" I could see the realization hit her before she even asked her next question. "Sam, did he set the fire that killed …?"

Staring straight into her eyes numbly and without emotion, I whispered, "Yes."

As if in a panic, she rapidly fired questions at me, "Are you sure? How do you know? Did he tell you? When did he tell you? Why did he tell you? For God's sake, talk to me!"

"Wait," I said, trying to slow the conversation down. After my heartbeat came back into my chest and I felt I could talk without sobbing, I said, "He told me and used it to threaten me …every time he took me to Grandma's basement."

She took a calming breath, let it out, and asked, "Sam, why did he take you to the basement?" Coach waited patiently as I mustered up the courage to reveal the secret that had haunted me for as long as I can remember.

Finally, I started to talk, "He called it hide and seek." I gagged at the thought and eventually continued. "He'd make me take my clothes off." I could feel her stiffen beside me. I continued, "He'd blindfold me, tie my hands behind my back, and force me to find what he'd hid on his own naked body."

Silently, I wept, and for several minutes she let me.

Gently, Coach said, "Sam, it's okay. You have to get it out." She wrapped her arms around me, and I fell into her, letting the sobs come uncontrollably. For several minutes we sat on the floor of the dirty locker room until my tears ran dry.

Without even realizing it, I heard my voice begin to sneak out of my body again. Completely overwhelmed by my emotion now, I shouted, "I had to! He said he'd burn me up if I didn't! Why? What did I ever do to him? I was just a little girl."

When silence overcame me, she gently whispered, "It's okay.... it's okay." She paused then asked, "Was he the man you saw in the window, hon?"

"I...I'm pretty sure. It looked like him." I answered.

"Didn't he disappear about a year ago?" she asked. "...right after he graduated from school?"

"Yeah, I guess." I shrugged. "I thought so."

"Is this the first time you've seen him since?" she questioned.

Keeping my answers short, I responded, "I'm not sure." In my heart, I knew he'd been creeping around. I could feel him somewhere in the background. Just the thought of his presence made my skin crawl.

CHAPTER EIGHTEEN

When I got home from practice that night, our driveway was full of cars. *I didn't know we were having a party,* I thought, and I headed to the door. Once inside, I was relieved to see that it was just a bunch of ladies from our church over to make cookies or something for the church bazaar that Saturday. Flipping off my shoes, I was extra careful not to make any noise so I could just silently slip to my room undetected by the nice but super-nosey ladies furiously baking in the next room.

Once safely in my room, I flopped onto my bed like a lazy fish and grabbed my closest friend, Charlie. As usual, I filled him in on the events of the day. When I got to the part about the barn, I felt scared all over again. Shutting my eyes and squeezing him tightly, I screamed as suddenly something heavy bounded onto the bed next to me.

"Oh, man! You jerk!" I shouted, swinging my beloved turtle at my dopey brother. "What the heck are you doing?" I shouted again as he continued to jump on my bed.

"Just bugging my fav little sis," he said as he finally did a seat drop to land on my bed, nearly smacking his head on the wall behind him.

Smacking him with my pillow, I laughed. "You're a dork!"

He grabbed the pillow from me and swung it back at me, "No, your face is a dork."

I dodged the pillow. Jumping off my bed and leaning into him, I said, "Your mom's a dork." We both burst out laughing, and I dove on the bed as he quickly rolled away from my body slam.

Lying there on our backs, staring up at the poster of Mary Lou Retton on my ceiling, he said, "Were you guys past the old barn before it started burning?"

Without looking at him, I answered, "We were in it."

Rolling up on his elbow he asked, "What the heck, Sam?"

Still not looking at him, I insisted, "Don't freak out." I paused then added, "I saw him."

Sitting up on my bed, he turned angrily toward me and whispered loudly, "Him? Are you sure?"

"Yeah," I said slowly sitting up too. "He looked right at me from the upstairs window."

"Oh my God, Sam. We have to tell someone," he spat out.

"No. I talked to Coach, and she's the only one who's going to know!" I half shouted back.

Standing up to face me, he said worriedly, raking his hands through his hair from front to back, "You have to be extra careful, and we have to really watch out if he's back. Promise you won't go anywhere without me until they find him or he bolts again."

"Duh," I said, trying to sound more annoyed than scared.

"Seriously, Samantha, he's dangerous. He's already killed, and I'm sure he won't hesitate to do it again." I could see the anger on Mark's face as he paced my room.

"Stay here. I'm going to talk to the guys. Maybe we can find him before he does anything else." Before I could protest, he was gone.

My nerves got the best of me, and I paced my room for nearly an hour, worried about what Mark was up to. I feared for him, as Monte once told me he'd be the first to go if I ever told anyone what he did. When I couldn't stand it any longer, I dug in my closet for some old tennis shoes and sneaked out my window on a mission to find either Mark or Monte, whichever came first.

Frantically, I slinked from yard to yard throughout our neighborhood. As I passed near structures, I peered carefully into each and every window, hoping to find a clue as to where Monte had been hiding out or where Mark went. I saw a light on in the Miles's garage and skirted around closely so as not to be seen. Once I was past, I wound my way through the tall bushes of the Madsens' yard and headed toward the haunted Becker house. As I got closer, I thought I saw something scurry quickly around the corner toward the windows we snuck in the night of the "burning poo" incident. Carefully, I approached the house, trying my best to stay absolutely silent. When I got closer to the basement window, I was sure there was a slight trickle of light coming from it. My heart was practically pounding out of my chest when I dropped to my hands and knees and crawled toward the window. Rocks and fallen tree branches jabbed painfully into my knees as I made my way toward the window. All of a sudden, something came around my head and grabbed my mouth and nose. I couldn't breathe, making it impossible for me to get air to scream. Terror flooded through me, and then I heard his voice.

"Sam, don't scream." My body went limp as I realized the voice attached to the hand clasping my mouth and nose was coming from Mark's friend, Seth.

"What the heck are you doing here, Mouse?" he demanded, letting go of my face, allowing me once again to breathe.

When my feet hit the ground and enough blood came back into my legs to hold me up, I turned toward him and punched him as hard as I could in the chest. "What the heck are you doing? You scared me! You jerk!" I screamed.

"Uh." He sighed and then reached out to put his hand back over my mouth, "Shut up, woman. You're going to get us caught."

Before his hand reached anywhere near my face, I slapped it away, "Don't touch me again! Next time you're getting it in the nuts!" I spat angrily right in his face.

He grabbed my arm and put his index finger in front of his lips, giving me a look that would kill. I decided it best I shut up at that point before he actually knocked me out to shut me up. When his grip relaxed on my wrist, he pointed to the window to let me know we were going in. Just as we dropped to a crouching position to slither through the window, Mark appeared behind the glass. Lifting it, he said angrily, "Both of you, shut up and get in here."

I inched my way through the open window, and as soon as I hit the floor, Mark laid into me, "Samantha, I told you I'd handle it. This is not a place for you!"

"I know you're pissed, but I couldn't sit home and wait, knowing that freak is out there!" I shot back.

Looking at Seth and Joe, he said, "Now what?"

They both shrugged their shoulders at my brother, and then all three glared at me as if they wanted to kill me.

I folded my arms in front of my chest and steadied my position firmly to the spot in which I was standing. "Too bad, I'm not leaving!"

Just then, Mark walked over to me and whispered, "Sam, I love you, but go home!" He turned back to Seth and Joe and said, "Hang here, guys. I'm going to take this little hemorrhoid where she belongs." Grabbing me around the bicep, he squeezed tightly and pushed me toward the open window.

"Mark, come on!" I protested as he forced me up through the dirty opening. "Let me stay...please," I begged. He followed me out, and together we worked our way home weaving between trees, cars, bushes, and fences so as to not be seen by anyone.

Neither of us said a word as we entered our yard. He just gave me "the look" and let go of my arm with a push toward the house. I got the message and headed back in the same way I sneaked out. When I looked back, he was already out of sight. The rest of the night, I listened intently for his return. Silence filled our house until sunlight began slipping into my open window. Then I heard a faint tapping noise.

I sprang out of bed and darted to the glass. Outside I could see Seth crouched like a cat just about to tap again. I cranked it open a bit and whispered, "Where's Mark?"

"That's what I was going to ask you," he whispered back.

"What? He's supposed to be with you," I said, cranking the window wider.

"We lost him out at the old barn…you know, the one that was on fire yesterday," he said quickly.

"Seth, he's not here. I listened for him all night. Turn around a sec," I said and reached for a pair of pants. "What do you mean you lost him?" I barked hastily, stuffing my legs into jeans and wrapping a rubber binder around the extra T-shirt that hung down past my butt. "Okay," I said as I reached for my dirty sneakers and slipped my feet into them. "Let's go before my parents get up." With that I slipped out my window, and Seth and I ran down the block to where Joe waited impatiently in the car.

As I reached for the door handle, I screamed, "Mark!" I couldn't get the door open fast enough. When I did, I dove in and threw my arms around my big brother's neck. Sobs came out of nowhere. He squeezed me hard and said, "Sam, what's the matter?"

Slightly loosening my grip, I slid my hands to grasp around his throat, squeezed, shook his head playfully, and said right in his face, "You big jerk! Where have you been? You scared the crap out of me!"

He reached up and, grabbing my puny wrists, gently pried my hands from around his throat. "Little sister, you have to trust me. I've been scoping out that freak. He leaned forward to see around me and said to his friends, "Come on, I'll show you where he's holed up."

Seth jumped into the back seat, and I climbed in beside him. As Joe pulled away from the curb, Mark turned around and said, "Man, this guy is nuts." Turning his vision to Joe, he added, "He's staying out in the old barn." He relaxed back into his seat and, looking out the side window, said, "I don't trust him. He's up to something."

CHAPTER NINETEEN

As tenth grade came to an end, Mark and the other distance boys were never far away as we ran our miles. Sometimes they'd even run with us and challenge us to races. It was an awesome season, and we had the boys to thank. Because of them, we were running times that were unheard of for girls' 800-meter runners. It was awesome, and for the first time, I really enjoyed school. The older girls were great to us younger ones, and the school thought of us as hometown heroes when we went on to kick some serious butt at the state track meet that June.

Not even a week after the state meet, I was off to gymnastics in the cities. For the first time ever, I was actually going to miss friends at my high school. Through all our trials and triumphs, Mandy, Mel, Liz, and I had gotten really close during the season. When we'd run, the four of us stuck together like glue, and it was nice that the boys were never far away. Heck, I'd actually developed a crush on one of them. He was in my grade, tall, dark, handsome, and totally hot. I think he noticed me too, at least I was hoping he did. More days than not, he'd run with me and not the boys. At first, I thought it was weird until Mandy and Mel started teasing me about it in the locker room.

As Mark and I were loading up the car for our annual road trip to summer gymnastics in Minneapolis, I was shocked when I heard a voice behind me say, "Hey, Sam. You leavin' already?"

Realizing it was my crush, Colton, I took a deep, calming breath, patted down my hair, turned toward the voice, and replied, "Yeah, it's time to be upside down for the next three months."

He stepped into our driveway, closing the gap between us. Mark noticed and said, "Hey, I have to get something inside…be right back." He winked at me over the top of the car, and I felt my face burn hot with embarrassment.

"So, you over here visiting Becky?" I asked, hoping he'd say no. I knew the two of them had gone out because she had made it a personal quest to tarnish every boy I'd ever mentioned I'd remotely liked. It was her little way of still being a jerk to me. Whatever, I was outgrowing her garbage and had learned to blow her off…most days.

"Nah, I heard you were leavin' today, and I thought I'd come say good-bye," he said sheepishly, stuffing his hands in his pockets.

"Who'd you hear that from?" I asked, stepping to a spot where I could lean up against the side the car. Folding my arms in front of my chest, I added nervously, "…and why would you want to come say good-bye to me?"

"'Cause," he said and took a deep breath stepping forward and leaning up against the car next to me. "I'm gonna miss you."

I was shocked, and for what seemed like forever, I stood there not knowing what to say. Suddenly, I lost control of my verbal filter and said, "Come see me."

"Really?" he shot back before I'd even realized what I'd said.

"Um…sure," I said, shifting my weight from one foot to the other and staring at the ground. "Why not? It'd be fun."

"Okay. When?" he said excitedly, stepping in front of me and away from the comfort of the car.

"Whenever," I said, looking him in those beautiful blue eyes. As I stared into those dreamy puddles, my attention was distracted by a sudden, dark, shadowy movement across the street. My breath caught in my throat, and he noticed something was different in my demeanor.

"What? Sam," he said, realizing the change in me. "What's the matter?" He kept on shifting his vision to match mine. I could see him squinting to see what it was that had startled me. "Hey, what did you see?" he asked.

"N ...nothing," I said too quickly, still staring across the street. "It was nothing." I continued shaking my head and looking back at him. "What were you saying?" without missing a beat I added, "Oh yeah, a visit, anytime. You have my cell, just call and tell me when you're coming. That'd be great." I was talking so fast, it was a mystery how he could keep up.

He reached out and grabbed my hands in his, "Hey, slow down. Do you want me to go see what's over there?"

"No. I'm just paranoid," I said, squeezing his fingers. "Too many weirdos for one year."

Not letting my hands go, he added quietly, "I'm not a weirdo, Sam. You're safe with me." Then he leaned in and kissed me gently on the mouth.

My knees went weak, and I had a funny, tingling feeling in places I didn't know I could have funny, tingling feelings. What was that? I wondered for a second and then let myself enjoy this amazing new feeling completely. He pulled away and said, "I'll call you. I promise."

Then as if he'd been waiting for the perfect moment, Mark slammed the door and shouted, "Put it away, buddy, I have to get this shining star to the cities."

Laughing, Colton shouted to my brother, "Okay, man! Do what you have to do." As he let my hands go, he said to me just loud enough for me to hear, "See ya soon." Then he winked and walked back in the direction he'd first appeared.

I watched him walk away and had to admit to myself that it was almost as nice as watching him walk toward me. Totally spellbound in watching Colton's jean's pockets distance themselves from me, I didn't even notice that Mark was standing next to me until he said, "…you think he has a nice butt?"

Embarrassed, I aggressively leaned into him, hard enough to knock him off his balance, and laughed as I moved to the passenger side of the car. Looking up over the top of our little ride, I said with a bit of a laugh, "Shut up and drive."

CHAPTER TWENTY

When mid-August rolled around and I hadn't had any signs of anyone from home, I wasn't sure if I was relieved or not. On one hand, I was relieved Monte hadn't followed me here this summer; but on the other hand, Colton hadn't shown up or called either. I guessed uneventful was better than the alternative.

All of this "uneventfulness" came to a screeching halt on the last night of gym. We'd had just had a great practice and celebrated an amazing summer with our annual end-of-the-summer party. It was the first time since May for some of us to actually enjoy the amazing taste of junk food. Our coaches were very strict about our diet during the summer, chips and pop being totally out of the question. However, this is the one night when they supplied us with what we had all missed over the summer. Chips, salsa, pizza, pop, chocolate, and all the other forbidden treats had never tasted so yummy.

When we had had our fill of empty calories, we continued our joyous conversations about the most awesome crashes and great new tricks we had experienced during the past few months as we hugged and said our good-byes. As everyone was leaving the gym, a scream sounded from somewhere around the corner of the building.

My teammate, Allison, who was leading the gaggle, slammed her arms out, clothes-lining all of us behind her, preventing us from taking another step forward and shouted, "What was that?"

Pointing to the left toward the north end of the building, I answered, trying to hide the panic in my voice, "I…I think it came from around there." I pushed her arm out of the way and moved stealthily toward the wall of the building.

"Sam, no…get back here," one of the other girls warned in a loud whisper.

Ignoring the warning, when I reached the wall, I crouched low and made my way to the corner of the building. I hugged the huge cement structure as close as I could to prevent creating a shadow as I drew nearer the end of the building. In the past few months, the streetlight had been a security blanket, but now was only a possible death sentence. Reaching the end of the wall, slowly, cautiously I slipped my head around the corner just enough to see. The hair on the back of my neck was standing up on edge, and I had a strange, tingling feeling in my legs. I prayed they wouldn't fail me if I needed to move fast. As my eyes focused to the darkness behind the building, I jumped straight as something touched me from behind.

"Oh my God, Allison, don't sneak up on me," I scolded instantly and way too loud.

"Safety in numbers…" she said, trying to get past me.

Pushing her back, I whispered, "Hang—" The rest of my sentence caught in my throat as a dark, shadowy figure bolted across an open grassy space between our building and the one next to it.

Allison saw it too and screamed. Without hesitation, I turned, grabbed her by the arm, and sprinted, dragging her along with me back to the door to the gym. As I ran, I noticed that the rest of the girls were crouched down behind one of the cars in the parking lot directly across from the main entrance. I shouted as loud as I could in the direction of my teammates, "Get in the building! Now! There's somebody back there, and I don't know where he went!"

Grabbing the front door of our gym, I yanked it open with such force that it made a loud crack as the commercial door closer snapped, ripping the handle out of my hands and causing the weight of the door to crash into the brick wall. Thankfully, it didn't shatter. Not even thinking, I yelled to the girls again as they scrambled toward me and into the door, "Hurry!"

When everyone had crossed the threshold, I violently pulled the now swinging door shut. Just as metal connected with metal, our coach reached over the top of me and, jabbing the key in the lock, turned it to safety. I could feel the air leave my lungs and the room as we all felt a rush of relief to be securely locked in our gym. Quickly, I moved away from in front of the glass door and dropped to a seat on the bench to my right with the others out of the line of sight from anyone outside. Cupping my head in my hands, I cried, "I'm so sorry."

Having a seat beside me and putting his hand on my shoulder, my coach said quietly, "Sam, why would you say that? You did great out there."

I shook my head as the tears dropped from my cheeks to the floor. Lifting my head to look him in the eyes, I said, "This is all my fault." I looked back down at the floor and slowly let all my breath out.

His hand rubbed soothingly on the back of my head, "We're safe. I already called 911 ...the police are on their way." As if what I had just said finally registered in his head, he added, "What are you talking about—your fault?" I felt his hand stop and his body stiffen. "Sam? Who was out there?"

Slowly, I sat up and leaned back against the wall. Before I could say anything, someone pounded on the door. "Police, open up!"

Forgetting about me, our coach leaned forward, making sure it really was a policeman. Once he had determined it was really the cops, he stood and moved quickly toward the door, opening it with his key.

As they entered the room, the big one said, "It's okay, girls. We've searched the area, and if there was anyone out there—"

Allison jumped up and interrupted, "If?" she huffed. "There was someone out there!" I grabbed her hand from where I was sitting and gave it a pull.

"Okay, calm down, honey," the cop said, stepping more into the middle of the front lobby, trying to get her to relax. "Whoever it was is gone now," he added in a soft voice. "We'll make sure each of you gets home safely and recheck the area in the morning." Turning to our coach, he said, "Coach, it might be a good idea to close up shop for a few days just to be safe."

Without hesitation, Coach replied, "Absolutely, Officer. No problem. It was our last night of practice for summer session anyway." Looking at us, he continued trying to lighten the mood, "At least this creep has good timing."

We all laughed at his totally inappropriately placed comment, and one girl said, "Leave it to Coach to drop a funny at the dumbest time."

"Yeah, yeah, yeah, get your stuff gathered up and get home before I get an itch to make you all do one hundred pull-ups before you leave," Coach said, giving us a huge grin.

"Pretty sure we covered that," one of the girls said, pointing at the broken door. "Mouse actually broke a hydraulic doorstopper."

As we all burst out laughing, the officer in the middle of the room reached out, gave my bicep a squeeze, and let out a long whistle. "Feels to me like she's right." Looking me in the eye, he added, "Nice pipes, little lady." He shot me a wink as he let go of my arm and started for the door. "Okay, all, time to roll."

In a couple of minutes, we were all in the parking lot hugging, laughing, and once again saying our good-byes as if nothing had happened. Finally climbing into my car, I felt a chill climb up my spine but tried with everything in me to keep a smile on my face as I closed my door, started my engine, and waved as I drove away for the last time this summer.

All the way home, I had that same horrid feeling that someone was following me. I couldn't shake it. Pulling into the driveway, I was relieved to see a crowd of people in the front yard. "What the heck?" I heard myself say over the blaring radio. Dread filled my heart. "Oh please, God, don't let them be hurt."

I pulled up and stopped in my usual spot. I took a deep breath and shut off the engine. Yanking the keys out of the ignition, I leaned over to grab my gym bag out of the passenger seat and nearly jumped out of my skin when someone stuck their face in front of the passenger side window. Realizing it was just my cousin, I stuck my tongue out at him and got out of my car. As soon as I rounded the front of my car and turned toward the crowd of people, they all yelled, "Surprise!"

Stepping cheerfully toward me my aunt shouted, "We thought we'd throw you a good-bye party!" Bouncing as she walked backward toward the front door, she added brightly, "Throw your bag inside and let's party!"

"You got it." I forced myself to laugh, not being able to help wondering in the back of my mind where my dreaded psycho cousin was hiding.

CHAPTER TWENTY-ONE

"Hey, Mouse!" I heard a deep, male voice yell as I entered our high school for the first day of eleventh grade. Before I even turned around, I knew who it was.

Turning toward the voice, I shouted back, "Hey, DJ!" As I made eye contact with my old friend, I saw a strange look cross his face. "What's that look for?" I asked as we met up in the middle of the street.

"Whoa, you look…" He let out a whistle and grabbed my shoulders, spinning me around in a circle.

I grabbed his arms when we came to face each other again. "Knock it off, weirdo. What's with you?" I asked.

"Nothing…" He hesitated for a few more seconds, scanning me up and down oddly. "You look different."

"Thanks," I said, thinking the worst. I gave him a shove and started walking away.

Catching his balance, he caught up to me. "No…I mean it in a good way," he said quickly as he walked beside me. "Oh, little mousey girl, I can't wait to see the look on Becky's face when she sees you."

Putting the death grip on his arm, I pulled him around the side of the building and asked irritably, "What the heck are you talking about?"

"Dude, have you not looked in a mirror in the past three months?" he asked.

"Of course I have, you dork," I said, beginning to lose my patience. "What's the big deal?"

"Mouse, you're not a little girl anymore. You look amazing," he said, grinning like the Cheshire cat, lifting his eyebrows up and down and whistling. Nodding his head he added, "Oh yeah, I'm totally walking in with you. I wouldn't miss this for the world."

Laughing at his "royal goofiness" and flexing my muscles at him, I said, "You just like my new pipes." With that I turned to walk back around the corner, secretly smirking to myself when who did I literally run smack in to? You guessed it. Colton, of all people.

"Sorry," I said nonchalantly and just kept walking into the school and up the stairs. I was nearly at the top of the first flight when DJ had caught up to me.

"Did you see his eyes pop out of his head when he saw you?" he blurted excitedly.

"Shut up," I said and kept walking.

"Seriously, Sam, his jaw dropped to his chest," he said, keeping pace with me. "It was awesome."

"So what? That jerk never even bothered to call all summer. Screw him," I said, dismissing the fact that Mr. Colton Mitchell had ever even existed. "He's a d-bag."

Laughing out loud, DJ teased, "Whoa, not only has our little girl gotten a new look, but she's gotten a new vocabulary too."

"Bite me," I said, teasing back as he pulled open the door to our hallway and acted like a servant bowing and waving his arm to let me pass first.

"Enter your kingdom, my princess," he said with an English accent.

I rolled my eyes at him as I passed through the door entering the junior hallway. I heard the door shut, but DJ was not at my side, when I turned around, he was walking a couple steps behind me. "What are you doing back there? Get up here, silly," I said.

"I'll wait…just enjoying the view." He sneered at me.

Stopping, I slammed my hands on my hips and stuck my butt out at him. "While you're back there, you could at least get used to kissing it." I laughed.

"Not a problem," he joked back, stepping toward me to close the gap between us. Giving me a slap on the hinder, he asked, "You gonna let me this year or is that reserved for King Colton?"

I growled at him and walked away in search of my new locker. Looking back, I added, "I think your locker is on the other end of the hall. Shoo, varmint."

He laughed as I walked away. "See you at lunch unless we have a class or two together."

"Oookay." I giggled back at him, secretly loving this completely foreign kind of male attention from, of all people, DJ.

I walked along the wall of lockers searching for the one with the number that matched the one on my schedule. Finally, near the end of the first row closest to the stairs leading to the gym, I found number 3-336, my own personal storage unit for the next nine months. As gently as possible, I put my loaded backpack on the floor next to me and tried the combination printed on my schedule. Slowly, I twisted the dial, stopping precisely at each number. Stopping on the last number, I paused a second and took a deep breath before pulling up on the latch. It actually worked the first time. Secretly, I prayed that was an omen of the year to come.

Pulling open the door, I screamed a deep, growling throaty noise that only came out of me when sheer terror took over my body. Dangling from one of the coat hooks was the charred remains of something that looked like it used to be a cat. Frozen, unable to move, I just stood there, trying to catch my breath.

"Samantha!" I heard someone call from what sounded like a million miles away.

I couldn't answer. My eyes were glued to the thing in my locker, and my vocal chords were paralyzed. Suddenly, I felt as if I was floating in air.

When I opened my eyes, I was in the nurse's office on one of her cots, and my mom was leaning over me.

"Sam, are you okay? It's Mom." I could hear her voice, but I couldn't make myself answer. What happened to me? Why wouldn't my eyes open?

"Honey, open your eyes." She softly commanded, but still my body wouldn't respond. Then the most putrid odor stunned my nasal passages, and I shook my head, coughed, and gagged on the scent.

"Oh, what?" I gagged out. Wiggling myself to a semi-seated position, I asked, "Where am I?" I rubbed my eyes and tried to focus on the voice in front of me.

"Samantha, wake up, sweetie." Now my mom's comforting voice penetrated the fog, and I looked at her, confused.

"Mom, what's going—," stopping midsentence, I instantly remembered what had happened and sat straight up on the cot. "Did you see it?" I shouted in her face.

Sitting beside me, putting her hand in mine, she squeezed and said, "Calm down. Yes. It's gone. The janitors took it out."

"Did you call the police?" I questioned.

Confused she asked, "Why?"

I looked her in the eye and said, "I'm pretty sure I know who did this."

She looked away and shook her head. "Honey, I'm sure it's just the girls trying to get your goat." She paused then added, "Principal Cabrillo is talking to the girls and their parents right now."

"But Mom—," I tried to interrupt.

"He'll take care of it," she insisted. "Trust us."

I didn't say any more. She wasn't going to believe me, and I was to blame for that.

Leaving the nurse's office, I headed straight for the bathroom. I wanted to wash my hands immediately. As I pushed the door open a bit, I heard someone inside mention my name. I stopped to listen, hoping to get a clue as to whether it was the girls or not.

"I can't believe that little freak got us in trouble the first day," I heard Becky whisper loudly.

"Ah, have you seen her yet, Bec?" Alexis shot back.

"No, why?" Becky asked.

"She came back with …" She paused. "Never mind, I don't want to spoil it for you." I could hear the devilish smile on her face even without seeing it. After a long pause, she started talking again. With obvious disgust in her voice, she said, "Did you see that nasty thing when they took it out of Samantha's locker?"

"Yeah, sick, huh? I can't believe they'd think I'd even touch something like that," Becky admitted. "Duh."

Just then, someone tapped me on the shoulder from behind. Startled, I jumped and turned to see Mandy standing there.

"What's going on?" she whispered, trying to see around me into the crack in the door. Pushing my head down, she whispered again, "Did you grow?"

Backing up, letting the door silently fall closed, I said, "Hey, long time no see."

She hugged me and asked again, "Sam, what's going on?" Not waiting for an answer, she pulled away and asked, "Who's in there?"

Putting my index finger to my lips, I took Mandy by the elbow and walked away from the bathroom door. When I felt we were far enough down the hall, I said, "It's Becky and Alexis, and I just heard them admit they didn't put that nasty burned cat in my locker."

Totally out of character, Mandy waved her two middle fingers in the air toward the wall with the two girls behind it and said with a head bob I'd never seen on her before, "Bull crap."

Silence was no longer an option. I couldn't stop the laughter from bubbling up and out as Mandy did her best gangsta dance. That's not something I'd ever heard before, and it was way too funny to even begin to try to hold back. "Wow! Where did that come from?" I laughed.

She turned back to face me, still in character with her hands on her hips, and continued, "Forget me, girl. Where did you come from? Look at yourself." She strutted in a circle around me, looking me up and down. When she came back around the front, she stopped, scanned me with her eyes once again, and putting her hand on her chin, said, "How am I supposed to call you Mouse looking like that?"

Exasperated, I let out a huge sigh. "What is everyone's problem with me today?"

"Sam, you have to admit that you've changed." She chuckled.

Sick of this line of discussion, I rolled my eyes and said, "Whatever."

"Whatever…come on, Sam, get real. You've grown about three inches, your hair is tons longer, no braces, make-up, and"—she pointed at my chest—"those are way past the nubby stage," she lectured, trying hard to keep a straight face.

Before I could even respond, we heard the bathroom door open around the corner. "Come on, let's get out of here," I said quietly.

"Amen," Mandy agreed. "Wanna buddy up in my locker 'till they get yours cleaned out?"

"Sure," I answered, and we took off down the hall.

When we got to Mandy's locker, I swung my backpack off my shoulder, letting it land hard on the floor. As I bent over to unzip the main pocket, I heard someone in the crowd of kids say, "Is that a new girl with Amanda?"

Apparently Mandy heard it too because she practically shouted, "Just stuff your bag in the bottom when you're done, Mouse. I've got to run."

"'Kay," I answered. I peeked up at her, giving her not only a headshake but a smirk that couldn't have said more if it had words attached to it.

She winked and took off down the hall. Turning back, she added, "Hey, if I don't see you it's 'cause I have to go to the dentist later, but I'll be back for practice." I looked up, waved, and before I could say anything back, she had been absorbed by the crowd.

Realizing I was going to be late too, I hastily forced my bulging bag into the tight little space at the bottom of her locker. As I slammed her door shut, I realized I hadn't asked her what the combination was. "Oh, buttmunch." I uttered under my breath.

"Big word, little girl. Heard you brought a pet to school," Mark said as he came up beside me.

"That was so sick." I grimaced.

"Becky?" he asked, concerned.

"Him," I whispered back.

When I lifted my eyes to meet his, I could not only see but feel the anger growing inside of him and decided it best to switch to the lighter side of this topic. "Mandy is letting me camp out in her locker until they get mine cleaned up, but I forgot to ask her the combo before she left."

"Which one is it exactly?" He asked curiously.

I pointed to 3-247, and a silly grin lit up his face. "Old buddy, old pal…"

As he was rubbing the locker and laying his face on it like an old girlfriend, I sighed. "You are one strange dude. Are you sure we're really related?"

Pulling me into a headlock, he gave me a noogie and said, "That's the one I had last year." He let go of my head and reached forward, twisting the combination first to the right then to the left. "Let's see if they change the numbers." As he stopped on the final number, he looked at me and said, "Drum roll, please." I thumped my fingers on his head as he jerked up on the latch. "Abracadabra!" he shouted and swung the door open.

Laughing at his dramatics, I said, "Okay, smarty pants, what's the combo?" He bowed in all four directions then scribbled the three magic numbers on the front of my notebook in obnoxiously giant hand writing, looked at me, grinned, and took off with Seth, Joe, and a couple of other guys as they passed by.

"Thanks!" I shouted in his direction, but he wasn't paying any attention, he was too busy giving Eric a dead arm.

"Shut up, Eric. My sister's off limits," Mark said as he hauled off and slugged his friend in the arm.

"Whoa, that's Samantha?" Eric said as he looked back, rubbing the sore spot on his arm and added, "Dude." Mark reached up and cuffed the back of his head, causing him to duck slightly and raise his hands in defense of any more attacks that might be coming. "Come on, man, wait," He pleaded when he saw Mark puffing up his chest, preparing to come at him again.

Getting in his friend's face, Mark said half joking, half serious, "Touch my sister and die, buddy."

"No worries man, Sam's one of the guys…always has been." Seth paused, shaking his head at Mark. "Girl got herself all growed up over the summer." With that he ducked past Mark and took cover on the other side of the Seth, Joe, and Neil.

Raising his hands to stop the messing around, Mark got serious, "Guys, you heard what happened to her locker, right?"

"Yeah," Joe answered and continued to walk toward the door heading to the gym.

"Becky's such a wench," Seth said as he pushed one of the double doors open.

Mark pushed open the other door and without even looking at Seth said quietly as he walked past his buddy, "It wasn't Becky." Nothing else was said about it the rest of the day.

CHAPTER TWENTY-TWO

Nothing else "interesting" happened the rest of the day. In fact, people seemed especially nice, which I wasn't going to complain about. Even Becky and her followers left me alone. Maybe that charred carcass in my locker scared them nice instead of stiff. Whatever the reason, I hoped it would stick.

As we were all sprawled out on the grass outside the gym, stretching for our run, Coach Simms came out and sat between Amanda and me. "I want you two to stick with the boys today," she said.

"Why?" I asked, afraid she'd actually answer.

"Yeah," Mandy added, "we're big girls." She shot me a look, and I sucked in air so fast that I couldn't help the loud snort that came out.

Throwing us a look of total understanding, she said, "I noticed." She paused. "But after today's incident, I think its best you stay in a group." She looked at me and continued. "Seriously, no wandering off."

"Okay," I agreed. Looking over at Mark and Seth, I couldn't help but to jab, "I hope they can keep up with us." They let out a moan and acted like they were hurt by my comment.

Coach got up off the grass, placed her hands on her hips, and ordered, "Now that that's settled, see you after five long miles." Looking right at the girls' team she continued, "And stay away from the old barn."

"Yes, ma'am," we all said in unison, like a team of army recruits.

"Okay, take off!" she shouted, echoing our army-style voices.

We all jumped up off the grass and began our run. At first I stayed next to Mark because secretly I was scared. Even though I hadn't seen Monte, I could feel him near, and it made my skin crawl. About three miles out, the boys started picking up their pace, and Mandy and I dropped to the back of the pack so we could still chat while we ran.

Falling in beside her, I panted, "Let's use these bozos to draft from, and then kick their butts at the end."

"Deal," she agreed. Together we hung at the back of the pack, saving energy and using the boys as a giant wind block. With about a half-mile left, I looked at Mandy and, without saying a word, we both took off. As we made our way through the pack of sweaty bodies, we talked to them nonchalantly, hoping to sneak our way to the front and break away before they could figure out what we were doing.

Mark was in front, as usual, and I think most of them thought I was just heading up to talk to him and Mandy was just coming along for the ride. However, Mark was not so easily fooled. As Amanda passed him on the left and me on the right, he knew instantly.

"So that's how you two want to play," he challenged. "You got it," he said and picked up the pace.

"Bring it, big brother!" I countered and kept up with him all the way to the school doors.

As we hit the grassy spot we started from, Mark leaned over putting his hands on his knees and laughed, "Whoa, Sammy girl, you picked up more than just new hooters and hair over the summer. You got some speed too."

Totally out of breath and trying not to puke, I responded as I put my hands behind my head and paced the sidewalk, "You should see my pipes." He laughed as he stood up and joined my walk.

"No way, I'm taking you on in a push-up contest." He reached over and grabbed my bicep. "You'd totally kicked my butt."

I looked at him, smiled, and then squinted my eyes tightly as I warned, "Don't you forget it either." With that I poked him in the chest with my index finger, walked past, and headed for doors to the gym.

Once inside, I took the familiar left and headed down the stairs to our private locker room. Mandy had gone straight in because she had to pee, so when I pushed open the door, I expected to see her standing there in all her glory. Instead, I found darkness.

"Mandy?" I called, "You in here?"

"Yeah," I heard an echo from back by the toilets. "Hold the door open so I can see where I'm going."

"Why are the lights off?" I asked, confused as I waited for her to appear.

As the words came out of my mouth, she came limping out of the darkness. "I don't know," she said as she closed the gap. "They were on when I came in, and as soon as I sat down to pee, it went pitch-black."

"You're limping?" I said inquisitively.

"My legs fell asleep."

I reached out and took her hand. Helping her to the door, I said, "Here, you hold the door, and I'll look for a switch."

"Be careful," she warned as I started feeling the walls all around the doorway.

I made my way around the back of the door and out of her line of sight. To calm my nerves I said, "There has to be something close to the door, you'd think." Suddenly my fingers went over something other than the smooth surface of the wall. I wasn't sure what it was, but I messed around with it. It felt like a hole in the wall, almost a box built into it. Just as I was about to stick my hand into the hole, the light flashed once and then came back on.

"Hey, you found it!" Mandy shouted cheerfully as she came back into the room, no longer limping.

"And you lost your limp!" I shouted back. As the door fell shut, I said in a more indoor voice, "Check out this wall."

"The switch?" Mandy asked as she came to inspect.

"Yeah, it's weird," I added, reaching my hand toward the odd hole in the wall.

"No!" Mandy screamed slapping my hand away.

Confused and rubbing the sting of her impact from my fingers I stuttered, "W-what?"

Stepping in front of the hole, she pulled herself together. "Someone has removed the cover on that switch, and those wires are obviously live."

"How would you know a wire is live?" I panicked.

"The lights are on, duh, so there has to be electricity going through them," she explained.

I backed away from the wall and sat down mindlessly on the bench, thinking of what could have happened. I ran my fingers through my hair, pulling out my hair tie, letting my hair fall back to my shoulders. As I shut my eyes and leaned my head back to shake it free, visions from my nightmares came screaming into my head. Startled by the images, I opened my eyes and shot to my feet.

"What's the matter, Mouse?" Mandy asked from in front of her locker. "You look like you've seen a ghost."

"Just a really long day…" I sighed, trying to calm my nerves. I walked over to my locker and fumbled my way through the combination, hoping Mandy wouldn't see my hand tremble. I couldn't help hesitate pulling the door open after what had happened just this morning. Slowly, I spun the lock to each of the numbers. When I settled the knob on the third and final number, I gave a soft yank; the door resisted. Pulling a little harder the second time, the sticky, upper-left corner stubbornly gave way, revealing the contents within. I let all the air out of my lungs and relaxed back to a sitting position on the bench when there was nothing there to greet me but my smelly, old gym bag. I grabbed the bag handle and pulled it out of the space. The zipper was still undone from before our run, so I just stuck my hand in and swooshed the contents around until I found my empty water bottle.

"I'm going to run and fill this up. Get dressed. I'll grab a janitor for the switch on my way back," I said as I stood, shaking my empty bottle in the air.

Jumping up from her spot, Mandy adamantly insisted, "No way you're leaving me down here by myself."

"Wouldn't think of it," I said as I pulled the door open for her. Together we made our way up the stairs, through the gym, and to the fountain. On our return trip, we saw Janitor Bob sitting on the stage watching girls' basketball practice.

As we approached the custodian, Mandy turned her head toward me and whispered, "What a perv."

I laughed and whispered back through my teeth, "Creeper."

Stopping in front of Bob, I was glad I had on a sweatshirt and not just my sports bra. From his point of view, he would have been able to look right down my shirt. Trying desperately to erase the thought from my head, I said, "Hi, Bob. Got a minute?"

"Yep," he answered, looking down at us. "What ya beauties need?"

Mandy jumped in with the details, "Someone took the light switch cover off the switch in our locker room and shut the lights off on me when I was down there. Can you fix it for us right now? I'm pretty sure those wires are live."

When he tipped his head down to look at her, his heavy, thick glasses slid down to the end of his greasy nose, causing him to have to squish his fat chin to his chest to be able to see. Once he'd inspected her thoroughly, he released the pressure off his vocal chords and said, "So now y'all are electricians, huh?"

"Please, Bob," I added quickly, knowing full well that Mandy was about to get irritated and that she was totally grossed out by this Janitor Blob.

"Okay, missy, I'm comin,'" he said and pushed all 250 pounds of him off his perch. Patting himself down, he said to no one in particular, "Yup, got my screwdriver."

For obvious reasons, Mandy and I followed at a safe distance. When we got to the bottom of the stairs, Bob pushed the door so hard it smacked against the wall with incredible force and noise. "Oops, don't know my own strength." He chuckled to himself.

Stepping into the room, Bob stopped so suddenly that both Mandy and I ran smack into the back of him. He grunted and said, "Girls, I think y'all should wait out there." It was too late; we were already in and saw what he was trying to keep from us. Written on the mirror in red paint or lipstick or something was the word "*BOOM!*"

CHAPTER TWENTY-THREE

I was going to ride home from school with Mark, but after what had happened in my locker and then in the locker room, the police made me go with my parents. The ride home was quiet. I think we were all talked out from answering questions for the past three hours at the police station. Finally, my dad said, "Don't worry, Sam. The cops are going to find him." Our eyes met in the rearview mirror. "I don't want you to be anywhere alone until they do though, 'kay?"

"That didn't seem to matter today." I sighed, dropping my eyes back to my lap. After a long pause, I asked, "Dad, what do you think he meant by 'boom'?"

I could tell he was either thinking or didn't want to say. He looked at my mom, and they stared at each other for a long time before he said quietly, "Honey, there is something we need to tell you about your cousin." He inhaled, exhaled. "Your mom and I think it's time. When we get home, throw your stuff in your room and come upstairs.

Frustrated and on the edge of anger I yelled, "You can't start a conversation like that and then tell me I have to wait until we get home!" I sat forward in my seat. "No way."

Turning just enough to see me out of his peripheral vision, Dad said softly, "Calm down, sweetie. I want your brother to be there too." He looked at my mom, "Do you have your cell?"

"Yes," she answered in a very subdued voice.

"Get Mark on the phone and have him hightail it home," he directed. She dutifully followed his orders, but I could see her hands shaking as she dialed. What was it that called for a family meeting of this magnitude? We never had family meetings…they were almost taboo at our house. Usually whatever Dad said was what it was.

Mom's voice invaded my thoughts, "It went right to voicemail. I'll try Seth's phone."

I listened as my mom called Seth. From my vantage point in the backseat, all I could hear was her asking if he'd seen him and did he know where he was going. From what I could tell, Seth had no idea where Mark was. Frustrated, Mom hung up the phone and turned to Dad, "The boys haven't seen him since he took off in his car after school. They said they didn't know where he was going, but that he was very upset."

I gasped, and dread filled my every fiber as I realized exactly where Mark had gone: the barn.

"Dad, go to the old barn!" I shouted, practically crawling over the seat to turn the steering wheel myself. "Hurry! I know where he is!"

"Sam, I'm not deaf," he said, pushing me back into the backseat. "What old barn?"

"The one on our four-mile path, you know? The one that started on fire last spring!" I couldn't talk fast enough, and it felt like my words were getting totally jumbled in my mouth. *Oh please, God, I've never had trouble being a blabbermouth before. Please don't let my lips fail me now.*

"Sam, are you sure?" he questioned doubtfully. "They've kept a pretty sharp eye on that place all summer, and there hasn't been any sign of activity around there since the fire." He insisted.

"That's 'cause he always follows me to the cities!" I shouted convincingly. Looking over to Mom, I yelled, "Call 911!" As my dad realized I knew what I was talking about, he hit the gas and repeated for my mom to call 911.

"Hang on, girls!" he shouted and cranked the wheel, taking the necessary right turn onto the old country road faster than he should.

From the front seat, I heard my mom let out a little scream as the back end of the car broke loose, and we fishtailed. Dad quickly got the car back under control and softly patted her leg, "It's okay. Trust me."

"There it is!" I shouted, pointing out the front window over the backseat. "Do you see Mark's car?" I asked.

Mom pushed me back with her left arm and scolded me, "Samantha, sit down before you get hurt!"

"I can't help it. I have to see," I insisted, grabbing onto the seat back and pulling myself forward onto the edge of my seat.

As we rounded the corner into the barnyard, I saw Mark standing on some old wooden boxes, stretching to look in one of the dirty windows. "There he is!" I shouted in my mom's ear again and almost decked her when I threw my arm out to point out her window. "Down at the other end...on those boxes," I continued.

"I see him," Dad said, leaning forward up against the steering wheel so he could see down to the far end of the barn.

"Don't honk," I warned. "We don't want to scare Monte off before the cops get here."

My dad sat back in his seat as he pulled up next to Mark's car. Without hesitation, he threw the shifting lever into park. Reaching for the door handle, he said, "I hadn't exactly planned on it, kiddo." He pushed his door open as far as it would go and climbed out. Then he leaned in and told us to stay put. I couldn't help but be annoyed by being left behind, but I knew my mom would be scared if I left her in there alone.

I'd never seen it before. In fact, I didn't even think it was possible, but as my dad rounded the front of the car, he broke into an actual trot. Seriously, it was almost a run.

"He's scared. I've never seem him run before," I said, watching him go.

"...me either," my mom added.

All of a sudden we heard what sounded like an explosion, and the car shook violently. I heard a sound come out of my dad that was completely foreign. It sounded like a bear growling.

Mom looked at me, horror filling her face as she screamed and reached instinctively for the door handle. "Mark!"

I flew across to the passenger-side back door and pulled the latch with all my might. The door swung open, and I literally fell out of the car onto the ground. It felt like it was still shaking, but when I got to my feet, I realized it was me who was shaking. Something was wrong. In the now silent countryside, I heard the most god-awful sound. I recognized my mom's voice and sprinted with all my might to where my parents knelt on the ground next to my brother's motionless body.

"No!" I sobbed as I fell next to Mark. "No!"

My dad started shouting orders like a drill sergeant. "Sami, lift up his chin and check in his mouth." Rhythmically he pressed his weight onto Marks chest. "One, two, three, four, five—blow! One, two, three, four, five—blow!" he commanded. This pattern went on for several more seconds when I lifted my head and said, "What's that?"

"Sami, pay attention! Don't stop," my dad ordered as he compressed Mark's chest with a perfect pace.

"Sirens," my mom said. "Thank God, sirens." She stood and ran to the road to help direct them to Mark. Luckily, every time 911 was called in our county, fire and rescue came automatically too.

Mom ran sideways next to the open window of the ambulance driver as he made his way over to us. I could hear her babbling on and on but couldn't make sense of anything she was saying. By the look on the guy's face, he couldn't either.

Thankfully the barnyard was strictly grass, and the ambulance pulled right up to us. The driver practically pushed Mom out of the way as he jumped out and helped get their gear from the back. Within seconds, they were swapping out with Dad and me with expert precision. Dad wrapped an arm around Mom and an arm around me as we watched the men work. Once they had him in what they considered a stable condition, they carefully placed him on to the stretcher and into the back of the ambulance. While they were loading Mark, we ran to the car. With the slam of a door, they were gone, and we were right behind them.

There must have been a lot of things happening in the ambulance, because we never went to the hospital; we went directly to the airport. A man directed Dad to pull up beside the ambulance, and a paramedic came running over to his window. Before the window was even two inches down, the paramedic shouted over the roar of the plane, "Mr. Nelson, We are taking your son directly to the Mayo Clinic in Rochester, Minnesota! Either you or your wife is allowed to ride with us, the other will have to drive!"

I don't think it sunk in right away what the man was saying, because we all just sat there. Then my dad broke the silence, "Honey, you go with Mark. Sami and I will drive down right now. It's only a few hours, and we'll go as fast as we can." When I looked down, I noticed he had placed his hand gently over hers.

From the driver's side window, the paramedic shouted, "Sir, we don't have time to wait!"

"Okay, my wife is coming with you," my dad yelled back. By the time he finished his sentence, my mom was already out the door.

Without looking back at us, she ran around the front of the car. The paramedic saw her coming and said to my dad, "We'll take good care of them, sir. See you there."

"Thank you," my dad said in return and rolled up his window.

The paramedic ran to catch up to my mom, and as our car started to move, my mom turned and blew us a kiss. I returned the gesture and laid my head on the back of the seat. Suddenly the wind came rushing in the driver's side window again, and I heard the same familiar voice I'd heard only a second ago. The paramedic was back.

"Sir, the pilot has offered to allow you and your daughter the option to fly with him if you'd like, but you have to hurry!" the man shouted. "We have no time to lose." He pointed toward the back of the car and added, "Back into that spot up next to the fence!"

Dad slammed the gearshift into reverse and shouted through the window, "Already done!"

Boarding the plane, the man looked at me in a way that made my heart sink. I didn't know what to think, so I just sat and prayed in my head with my eyes shut for the next forty-five minutes.

CHAPTER TWENTY-FOUR

When we arrived in Rochester, Mark was taken directly to surgery, and a hospital liaison got us settled in a room that had futons, blankets, and a mini-kitchen that was stocked with fruits, raw veggies, ingredients to make sandwiches, and plenty of beverages. It was like our own little apartment right in the hospital. Pain filled my heart as I realized this room was reserved for families who were in for a long haul.

Time passed slowly as we waited for news…any news. We did our best to stay busy. Dad and I were in the middle of a game of chess, and Mom was in the bathroom when the door finally swung open, and a small woman with dark, walnut-shaped eyes, dressed in scrubs complete with hat, booties, and an untied mask hanging around her neck came striding in. Without hesitation, my dad sprang to his feet and stepped toward her. Before even taking a breath, he blurted. "How is he?"

The woman motioned for him to sit down. Quickly, I slid over to the far end of the couch as Dad perched himself precariously on the edge. Hastily, he said, "Sam, go get your mother."

I hopped up and headed for the door. Just as I tugged on the handle, my mom pushed from the other, and she fell in as I fell back. "What is it?" she asked as she regained her balance. Then her eyes left me and scanned the room. Panic set in at the sight of the medically dressed woman, and Mom's voice took over, "How is he? Who are you? What's going on? For God's sake, say something!" The volume of her voice grew significantly as she fired her questions in rapid succession. Fear molded itself on her face as she stepped deeper into the room.

Standing as she reached forward and took Mom's hand, the woman calmly said, "Mrs. Nelson, I'm Dr. Kumada. Please sit down."

As the doctor guided her to the couch, Mom's eyes nervously darted from the doctor, to dad, to me, and back to the doctor. Lowering herself to the couch, she stuttered softly, "I...I'm sorry. How is my son? How's Mark?" I saw her eyes fill with tears that threatened to spill onto her cheeks but hovered as she waited for the doctor to speak.

Once we were all sitting, Dr. Kumada instinctively reached over, pulled up an ottoman, and positioned it directly in front of the three of us. Her voice was mellow and thick with a hypnotic foreign accent. "As you may know, Mark has sustained significant internal injuries. During surgery, my staff and I had to remove his spleen, appendix, and left kidney." My mom gasped beside me, and I felt her fall into my dad. His arm came up and wrapped around her shoulder. She reached over, took my hand, and squeezed.

Tears were burning my eyes, but I couldn't let them see. I needed to be strong for my parents. I took a huge breath, held it for a second, and then tried to let it out as quietly as possible. The doctor continued, "Right now he's stable. However, I want you to know I have called in our chief neurologist, Dr. Taniguchi, to assess Mark's brain injuries. The blast has caused a bleed, and we need to find out where before we can operate."

When the doctor stopped to take a breath, my dad asked, "When will we know?"

Dr. Kumada softly said, "Dr. Taniguchi is getting scrubbed as we speak. He's the best neurosurgeon in the field. We should know something in the next few hours. One of my nurses will be coming in to visit with you as the surgery progresses." She paused. "Do you have any questions?"

"How long is 'a few hours'?" my mom whimpered.

"That I can't say for sure, but the nurse will keep you updated." She stood, and so did we. As she was leaving, my dad softly said, "Thank you." And then the doctor was gone.

As if possessed by some unknown force, I grabbed the door handle before it thumped shut and ran down the hall quickly, catching up to Dr. Kumada. Not caring at all if I was out of line or not, I grabbed her arm and pleaded, "Is he gonna die?"

Without so much as a blink, she wrapped her arms around me and whispered in my ear, "Not if I can help it, honey. You have my word." Finally I let a tear fall, then another, and another. She held me for a couple more seconds, and then as she loosened her grip, added, "I have to get back to him now, sweetie."

"Okay," I whispered, thinking to myself that this was the most amazing doctor in the world. "He's my hero, you know."

She smiled and replied, "All the more reason for me to get my butt back in there." Putting her hand on my shoulder, she gave it a reassuring squeeze. "I'll have him ready for his Superman costume before you know it." She turned and hastily strode back through the double doors leading to the operating rooms.

"Deal!" I shouted after her before the doors closed. With a newfound confidence, I headed for the ladies' room to pull myself back together before going back to Mom and Dad.

Why is it the brain goes into overdrive the minute bare cheeks hit cold ceramic? Maybe it's the temperature shock. I don't know. Whatever it was, it hit me like the burn your tongue experiences when stuck to a frozen metal pole. Instantly, the image of what got us here in the first place plunged into my brain. "Monte," I said out loud, startling myself.

Two seconds later, I blasted through the door of our "family room," startling my parents. I snatched up Mom's phone and hollered, "Be right back!"

Before I got to the end of the hall, I had already dialed DJ's number. Relief engulfed me when he picked up on the second ring. "Hey, Mouse," he said cheerfully. "How's my favorite rodent?"

Dumbfounded by his playful attitude, I demanded, "DJ, have you been veggin' out locked in your room with Metallica screaming in your head since after school or what?"

"Oh yeah," he answered, giving it his best effort to sound like a stoner.

"Idiot!" I exclaimed. "Shut off that crap and listen. I need you. Now!"

"Okay, okay, settle, little one," he said as I heard the music in the background abruptly disappear. Focusing his attention back on our conversation, he asked with concern, "What's up? You sound—"

"Mark's been blown up. I need you to—"

Now it was his turn to interrupt, "Whoa, wait a minute. Mouse, did you say 'blown up'?"

"Yes," I answered, "and I need you to go see if the police found Monte."

"Monte blew up Mark?" he questioned, obviously confused.

"I didn't stutter. Mark's in surgery right now, and I need you to find out if Monte has been caught." As I spoke into the phone, I paced the sterile corridor and cautiously scanned the halls of the hospital.

On the other end, DJ ordered, "I'm not going anywhere until you tell me what is going on!" Knowing DJ the way I did, I knew he wouldn't budge unless I spewed everything. "Sam, spill it." He demanded again.

As I filled DJ in on every detail of the past few hours, I walked and kept a cautious eye out for anything or anyone coming in my direction. The last thing I needed right now was someone sneaking up on me. With my nerves on such high alert, I wasn't sure what I would do if someone startled me.

After several minutes of nonstop word vomit, I took a deep breath and sighed into the phone, "So, that's how we ended up at Mayo and why Mark's in surgery."

"Holy crap," DJ said quietly on the other end.

"Double holy crap," I added, echoing his tone.

After a brief pause, DJ perked up and commanded, "Okay, you hang tight and keep this phone on you. I'll go see what I can dig up and call you back."

Unable to hide my relief, I said, "Thanks, D. You're the best."

Before snapping his phone shut, he bragged, "Gotta love me." And then he was gone.

For a few seconds, I stared at the phone in my hand and thought about the significance of the favor I had just asked of a dear friend. As I prayed for his safety, I was startled by the dinging of the elevator as it stopped to let off passengers just around the corner from where I stood. Before anyone emerged into the hall, I quickly tucked Mom's phone back into my pocket and took off toward the family room.

Once there, I pushed open the door and went straight for the fridge. Having DJ on the job settled my stomach enough to actually feel hungry. Once my masterfully crafted, mile-high sandwich was complete, I grabbed a napkin and a bottle of water and plopped myself down on the couch next to my dad.

"Nicely done, Sam," he said as he eyeballed my tower of scrumptious nutrition. I gave him my best smirk and smashed the masterpiece into my mouth.

Reaching out as if to steal it from me, he teased, "Hey, I thought that was for me."

Through a gob of meat, cheese, mayo, veggies, and bread, I ducked away from his hand and mumbled, "Not in this life time, buddy." I tucked a piece of meat that dangled from my lip back into my already too full mouth with my index finger and continued, "Get your own."

Laughing as he stood, he said, "Wow, who taught you to eat?"

"You," I teased back, trying to kick him in the butt as he passed in front of me on his way to the kitchenette. From the other side of the room, Mom chimed in, "Hey, I'll take one too, please." Smiling at my dad, giving him the old puppy eyes, she added, "Honey."

Just then, the phone in my pocket began singing Mozart's Fur Elise. Setting my dinner on the seat cushion beside me, I took a quick swing at dad and as he jumped out of my reach. Laughing, I said, "Saved by the bell." Then I fished the singing square out of the front pocket of my sweatshirt. Before answering it, I looked at the caller ID and saw that it was one of mom's friends.

"It's for you," I said, trying to hide the disappointment I felt that it wasn't DJ with news. After handing her the Blackberry, I sat back down and began working on my sandwich once again. As the final bite slipped down my throat, I patted my tummy and with defeated sleepy eyes muttered, "Uncle."

They both looked at me, and my mom said, "Honey, now that your tummy's full, you should lie down for awhile and try to get some rest before the nurse comes back."

"Shouldn't she be coming any minute?" my dad asked, looking inquisitively at her. She shrugged her shoulders, and I saw a look of fear and sadness pass between them. Realizing I was watching and probably saw the look, Dad made a surprise attack by smacking me in the gut with one of the throw pillows from the couch. "Yeah, go to sleep and quit buggin' me."

Grabbing the pillow and tugging it away from him, I said, "You just watch your goofy cowboy and Indian show and mind your own business." Then I stuffed the pillow under my head and waited for the peacefulness of sleep to take over my tired body.

CHAPTER TWENTY-FIVE

As I stretched, trying to wake up from my sleep, I discovered that my mobility was restricted. "What the heck?" I said out loud, opening my eyes and feeling pain shoot though my wrists and ankles as I struggled against my shackles. I cocked my head up and to the left. Panic began to bubble over in me the moment the reality of my situation sunk in. I was once again tied, spread eagle, on an old stained mattress somewhere in the man's barn. Instinctively, I began to pull and twist against my restraints. Then I heard something moving in the darkness.

"Who's there?" I shouted out. "Come on, show yourself!" Anger had taken the place of fear, and I felt a surge of courage rush through me.

An evil laugh came out of the darkness, and then he emerged into my field of vision. This time the man had a face I recognized. "Monte," I said loud enough for only me to hear.

He read my lips and replied, "The one and only." As he walked around to the head of the mattress, I felt him staring down at my naked body. Anger took over my mouth, and I blurted, "What's the matter, sicko, too chicken to look me in the eye?"

"Hardly." He sneered as he landed in a kneeling position straddling my head. Shutting my eyes, I wished with all my might to take back what I'd said, but it was too late. "Sicko, huh, let's see just how long it takes you to get sick." As he spoke, I heard the jingling of metal from above my head. I lifted my chin to see what he was doing.

"No," I screamed when I saw him undoing his belt and sliding down his zipper.

"Yes," he whispered with a demonic grin. As he leaned over me, I gagged, and he warned, "If you puke on me, brat, I'm gonna burn you where you lay."

Silently I cried, trapped under his weight, trying to hold my breath until I died. I must have passed out because the next thing I knew, I was coughing uncontrollably. Pulling against my restraints, I felt heat rising up from under me. From somewhere in the room, I heard Monte's sinister laugh. Twisting my head side to side, I searched for whatever was causing the burning sensation I felt in my feet. Seeing flames shooting up from the end of the bed, I frantically kicked my feet and screamed, "Help!"

Just as I thought I was going to die, something cold touched my foot. Opening my eyes, I lifted my head to see my dad sitting at the end of the couch, squeezing gently on my feet. "Hey, wake up," he said. "You're kicking me."

Sitting up onto my elbow, trying to shake the realness of what I had just dreamed from my head, I said, "Sorry, Dad, bad dream."

"I guess," he said. "You knocked my coffee right out of my hand. Wasn't it hot on your feet?"

"A little," I said quietly as I laid my head back down. Memories flooded my brain uncontrollably, and I shivered when I realized the dream had manifested because of what had happened to Mark today and what Monte had done to me all those years ago. Right now it felt like yesterday, but I was only about three years old. My grandma was out buying groceries, leaving Monte and me home alone. She wasn't aware of the evilness that took over his being sometimes. I remember him watching out the front picture window, watching her leave. When he was sure she wasn't coming back for awhile, he took me out into the woods, tied me to my wagon with rope he'd stolen from the garage, and did things to me that no little girl should ever have to experience. When he finished, he tried to burn me by lighting a fire underneath me.

"Thank God for Grandma," I accidentally said out loud, causing both of my parents to look up from what they were doing and stare at me.

"Where did that come from?" My mom asked.

"I…just thinking," I stuttered, trying to figure out a way to defuse the questioning.

From behind me I heard the door open and relief flooded through me. "…and thank God for nurses," I said quickly as I swung my legs to the floor and looked at her in anticipation of good news.

"Hello, Mr. and Mrs. Nelson," she said, settling herself on the same stool the doctor sat on before. Looking at me, she smile and added, "…and Samantha."

Dad's patience wore thin, and he interrupted her pleasantries by blurting, "How's my son?"

Feeling his urgency, she quickly got to the point. "The surgeons are just closing now. Mark did suffer a slight tear in his carotid artery, but they were able to patch it. However, before they were able to patch it, he did have significant bleeding in the brain, and the next seventy-two hours will be very critical in his recovery." Mom, Dad, and I were silent as we tried to process exactly what she was saying. She kept talking, "As for the internal injuries, like Dr. Kumada said before, we took out everything he could do without, patched the rest, and stopped his internal bleeding. Mark will never miss the organs that were removed, but his diet may need to be modified. Time will tell." She paused and then looked at my parents, "I hope you know how lucky your son was."

I could see tears well up in dad's eyes, and all he could do was shake his head up and down. The nurse took his hands into hers and said gently, "He has angels on his shoulders…and three more waiting for him to get better." After holding dad's hands in hers for a couple more seconds, she quietly stood and asked, "Are you all comfortable? Can I get you anything before my shift ends?"

Both my parents stood, and Dad said, "Thank you. We're fine."

The nurse left the room, and Dad and I sat back down on the couch. Mom walked over to the door and said, "I'm heading to the ladies room to brush my teeth. Sam, you probably should join me." Holding the door open, she smiled and said, "I mean, come on, that sandwich had more than a couple of onions." Then she waved her hand in front of her face, smiled, and walked out, letting the door fall shut behind her.

"She's got a toothbrush?" Dad looked at me and asked.

"Yeah, there's a bunch of them in the drawer over there," I said, pointing to the kitchen.

"Cool," he said as he stood and headed in the direction of my finger. "I'm in."

Laughing and joining him in the kitchen, I gave him a punch in the arm, and he pretended it knocked him off his balance and stumbled to the side. "Ah ha," I said as I stabbed my hand into the drawer grabbing the purple toothbrush. Plaque weapon in hand, I jumped into my best fencing stance and yelled, "*En garde!*" Before my dad could retaliate, I bolted for the door and headed to the bathroom.

As I hurried down the hall, I heard the sound of Mom's ringtone coming from the door that was just about to close behind me. Stopping, I turned abruptly, practically knocking over a laundry cart and an old Asian man pushing it. He shook his head at me in disgust, and I sprinted around him before he could scold me. Just as I pushed open the door to our room, I heard Dad say, "Sorry, DJ, she just went to brush—"

"I got it, Dad," I said and snatched the phone from his hands.

Dad shook his head at me and said, "Whoa, okay. No problem. I know when I'm not wanted." He tried to act hurt as he left the room.

As soon as the coast was clear, I spat into the phone, "Hey, it's me. What'd you find out?

I could hear the excitement in his voice as he spoke, "They got him, Sam." I didn't know it at first, but Mandy was in on a three-way, and she cheered into the phone. She must have gotten in on the recon mission. "He fessed up to everything, even killing his parents."

My dream shot back into my head, and I prayed nobody knew what he'd done to me. Fearful of the answer, I asked the question anyway, "Everything?"

"Yeah, the bomb, the cat, the fire in the barn, stalking you in the cities, and setting his own house on fire with his parents sleeping inside. It's all over the news." He paused to swallow and take a breath. "Turn on the TV. There's a giant cowboy-looking guy with a handlebar mustache and a ten-gallon hat called Officer—no wait—Detective Renner or something like that on telling about how they busted him! That scumbag is going away for a very long time."

Mandy jumped in, "Yeah, and the creeps in juvie are going to introduce him to a broomstick with slivers!" We all chuckled and cheered.

As we laughed, I reached for the remote started surfing for a local channel. "Hey, it's on. I found the news story." A picture of the old barn flashed across the screen, and I lifted my finger off the button. "Oh my God," I stared at the set. "Are you watching it too?"

"Yeah," they said in unison, obviously concentrating on what the reporter was saying. Several minutes passed as we all watched the same news story from two different venues.

"Hey, I hear my parents coming back from the bathroom. Call ya back tomorrow," I whispered, turning to look at the door. "Mandy, have you talked to Danielle?" I quickly asked.

"No, want me to call her?" she offered.

"That'd be great," I said. "If she sees it on the news before I tell her, she'll freak."

Genuinely, Mandy said, "Already done, my friend. You take care."

"Thank you," I said as I heard her click off her phone.

"D, you still there?" I asked.

"Yep," he answered.

"Thanks for everything. You guys are the best. Love ya, man," I said.

"Love ya too, Mouse," he replied.

As I snapped the phone shut, I heard my parents' voices just outside the door.

As they came into our little apartment, my dad's eyes focused on the TV across the room, "Sam, isn't that the old barn where Mark had his accident?"

"Yeah! I just talked to DJ and Mandy. You'll never guess what?" I blurted, jumping up and down.

"What?" they both said in unison.

I stopped bouncing and, pointing at the TV, said cheerfully, "They caught Monte, and he confessed to all kinds of stuff. The cop the reporter just talked to said they have enough to put him in juvie until he's twenty-one or maybe even enough to charge him as an adult now since murder is involved."

"Murder?" my dad asked as they mindlessly continued into the room, and we all sat together on the couch. Our eyes were glued to the TV as we watched the rest of the report together in silence. When a commercial break came on, they looked at each other and then back to me. Tear-filled eyes needed no words to express the relief we were all feeling.

"I should call my mother," Mom said concerned. "I'm sure she's confused."

Before she could find her phone, the report came back on. As we sat like zombies staring at the TV, we didn't even hear the nurse poke her head in the door. "It's okay to go in if you'd like to see Mark for a few minutes."

Unconsciously, we all looked at each other. Our brains were swimming in a pool of information overload, and we were having trouble registering what she was saying. The nurse saw the news story on the television and understood what was happening. She said, "Is that the guy who did this to your family?

"Yes," my dad answered matter-of-factly.

As if she could hear the roar in our brains, she said comfortingly, "I'm glad they caught him." We all sat quietly for a few seconds, watching the end of the news report. Then Dad looked at the nurse and said calmly, changing the subject back to her original reason for the visit, "You said something about seeing him now."

Turning her attention back to the three of us, she smiled and said, "Yes, but I have to tell you, he's swollen and bruised, but he's sleeping comfortably. Dr. K. has him is an induced coma, so he's not feeling any pain."

Cautiously, we got up and followed her into the intensive care unit. Leave it to my dad to say something dorky in hopes of lightening the mood. As we were entering the ICU, the nurse pointed to a plastic box on the wall and said, "Please scrub your hands with some sanitizer before entering."

We all made our way down the hall to Mark's room. The doctor was in the room pulling Mark's eyes open and flashing a light into them as we entered. He looked up as we came to the bedside. "He's hanging right in there, guys," he said with a smile. "We've done what we can. The rest is up to him."

Dad made eye contact with the doctor and said nothing. He looked down and picked up Mark's hand and held it in his. Then he spoke, not taking his eyes off his heavily bandaged, bruised, and swollen son. "He's a tough kid. He'll be home before we know it."

I squeezed my way in between my dad and the bed, forcing Dad's arms to comfortably encircle me. Placing my hand on top of Dad's hand, I felt movement. Surprised, I looked and my dad and said, "Was that you?"

"No," my dad answered. "It was him. He knows we're here."

I looked at the doctor on the other side of the bed and asked, "Why is he all puffy?"

The doctor explained, "It's just his body healing itself. The process isn't always pretty. He'll go through many different stages of inflammation and color changes. Just like when you get a black and blue mark.

"Got it. Can we take pictures so I can give him crap when he gets better?" I asked, and the doctor noticed my mischievous smile.

"Ah, I was a little sister too, and I see you are aware of your duties," she said as she lifted one eyebrow at me and grinned. "Okay family, it's time to let this big guy rest, and you all should get some sleep too. He's going to need you all strong and rested when he wakes up." She paused, and as we were walking out of the room together, she added, "This is going to be a long recovery, so take advantage of your time to rest and get plenty of nutrition."

As we were leaving the room, my mom paused and turned back to the doctor. Quietly she asked, "How long do you expect his recovery to be Dr. Kumada?"

Putting her hand on mom's shoulder, she answered, "It's going to be awhile. He's had a lot of trauma." Stepping out of the room, the doctor added, "Don't worry. He's in good hands."

Just then, the overhead intercom system sounded, and Dr. Kumada was paged to another location in the hospital. She sighed and said, "Sorry, duty calls." And she was off on a brisk trot down another corridor and out of sight.

CHAPTER TWENTY-SIX

I awoke the next morning to pop music in my ear. I had forgotten I'd put Mom's cell phone under my pillow after I'd changed her ring tone last night. Hurrying so as to not wake my parents, I hit the mute button, jumped to my feet, and as silently as I could, sneaked out into the hall. Once away from the room, I anxiously flipped open the phone and checked the caller ID. DJ's number popped up. A rush of adrenaline pumped through my body, and I hit the dial button. I couldn't wait to hear what was happening back home.

"Hey, Mouse, how goes it? How's Mark?" DJ said, instead of the typical hello I usually heard.

"We got to see him last night. He looks kinda creepy," I said quietly into the phone.

Sounding concerned, he asked, "What do you mean by creepy?"

"He's all puffy and bruised," I answered. "And he has this goofy stocking cap on to cover the hole in his skull."

"Hole?" he asked curiously.

"Yeah, they took a chunk of his skull out to allow for swelling in his brain. Gross, huh? They have it in a freezer."

"Okay, that is creepy. He awake?" DJ asked.

"No, Dr. Kumada has him in an induced coma so he won't move or feel pain," I assured him.

"How are your parents?" DJ asked.

"Okay, tired," I answered. "Dr. K said the next seventy-two hours will be the worst, then we'll be able to tell more." Not being able to stand it one more second, I shot back the question I'd been dying to ask since I called. "What's going on there?" Before he could answer, the phone in my hand beeped loudly in my ear. "Oh crap, I have another call. Hang on a sec while I see who it is," I said, annoyed. Looking at the little screen, I saw a number I recognized. Hastily I spat into the phone, "Hey, D, I'll call you right back. It's that Detective Renner guy. How'd he get this number?"

"'Kay, 'bye," I heard him say, and I hit the green button once again.

"Hello?" I said urgently into the phone.

"Mrs. Nelson?"

"No, this is Samantha. Is this really Detective Renner from the news show? What's going on?" I asked way too loudly, only to be shushed by a passing nurse.

"I need to speak to one of your parents, Samantha," he said officially.

"Okay. Give me a sec," I said as I sped back to the room, glaring at the cranky nurse as I flew past her station. I really wanted to give her the finger but settled for a dirty look instead.

Blasting into the room, I shouted as I jabbed the phone at my dad, "Dad, it's that Detective Renner. He has to speak to you right away!"

Taking the phone from me, Dad rubbed his face and head, trying to wake up enough to comprehend what was going on. "Hello?" he said deeply into the cell, stretching his legs.

"Mr. Nelson, sorry to wake you, but I thought we should touch base." I was thankful the cop had a loud voice. I could hear him clearly even though I wasn't on the phone.

"No problem, what can I do for you?" Dad replied.

"I just wanted to inform you that we have the perpetrator in your son's accident in custody and he's being held on $500,000 bond." The cop took a breath that resulted in an awkwardly long pause. Then he added, "I …I understand Monte LeReaux is a relative."

"Yes, he's my wife's cousin," Dad offered.

Delicately the detective continued, "I'm deeply sorry, sir, but we will need to see you, your wife, and your daughter for questioning as soon as possible. Would it be all right with you if I came to the hospital to visit?"

It was obvious to me that Dad was trying to control his voice, but he failed miserably when he said, "Of course, Detective. We want to do everything we can to put this scumbag away for a long time…family or not." Anger contorted Dad's face into something I'd never seen before. He was usually totally in control of his emotions. Then he growled into the phone, "What are the chances of this prick getting the death penalty?"

Ignoring Dad's tirade, Detective Renner calmly said, "First things first, Mr. Nelson. I'll be there later today."

"I'm sorry for ranting, Detective. Thank you. See you then," Dad responded and hung up the phone.

Wanting to get back to DJ, I impatiently blurted, "Dad, can I have the phone back?"

Focusing his attention on my mom, he absent-mindedly handed me the Blackberry as he relayed the conversation he just had with Detective Renner. I heard her begin to speak as the door went shut behind me, and I headed to my usual "call zone."

DJ picked up on the first ring. "…must have been waiting with your finger on the button," I said before he could even say hello.

"What'd the cop say?" my friend asked curiously.

"He said Monte's in jail and being held for half a mil." I couldn't help but let out a snicker. "No way that freak can come up with that. He's toast, or if my dad has his way, he'll be burned toast."

"No kidding," DJ added happily.

I couldn't stop my mouth, "…and get this, the detective said they're going to push to have him tried as an adult since murder is involved."

Stunned, DJ asked, "Can they do that?"

"I guess," I answered, sounding confused myself. Remembering what Dad had said I asked, "Does Wisconsin have the death penalty?"

After thinking a second, DJ answered, "I'm not sure. I'll check it out."

Getting back to the cop, I said, "Detective Renner is coming here this afternoon to question us."

The protector in my friend came flowing out, and he offered calmly, "Want me to come?"

I paused and then humbly added, "Yeah." I took a breath, trying to hold back the tears that burned the back of my eyes. Almost in a whisper, I asked, "Do you think you could maybe bring Mandy too?" I wasn't sure if that was okay with my parents, but frankly, I didn't really care. They had each other, and I wanted my friends.

"Sure, Mouse, anything for you," he said quietly. "I have to get things okayed with my parents and then at school first. I'll see you as soon as I can." Then he was gone.

I stared at the phone, dropped into the big squishy armchair, pulled my knees up to my chest, and let the tears come. I think it was relief that overwhelmed me, but with everything that was happening now and had happened in the past coming to a head all at once, I just needed to release some of the pressure. For several minutes, I had myself a good cry.

Once I felt like I could face the world again, I went into the bathroom and splashed some cold water on my face. After a nice head soaking, I made my way back to our room, where I found my parents on the couch all snuggled up and smooching. "Come on you two, get a room," I tried to joke.

Startling them both, my dad smarted back, "Hey, kid, I just can't keep my hands off your gorgeous momma." Then he winked at me and scooped her up in his arms. Standing, they twirled several times before he dipped her and laid her gently onto the floor. From on top of her, he looked up at me and smiled, "How'd ya like that move?"

"Ew," I screeched! "You two are so gross," I said, trying to sound appalled. Secretly, I loved that they still loved each other so much.

Dad looked down at Mom, gave her a big smooch, and then rolled off and sighed, "Whoa, that's too much for an old man to handle."

Seeing my opening, I jumped into the air, landing in a giant body slam right on him. I joked as all my weight slammed into his belly, "Can ya handle this, old man?" Mom saw me coming and quickly rolled to safety. Laughing, Dad and I wrestled on the floor until once again, the phone blasted my favorite song from my front pocket. Rolling over onto the floor, I stabbed my hand into my pocket where Mom's cell hid.

"Sam, what on earth did you do to my phone?" my mom said from the safety of the other side of the room. "Holy cow," she laughed, "that's gotta go."

Checking the caller ID, I defended my music choice by saying, "Hey, it's a good message, and we all needed something positive." She couldn't argue with that. Shaking her head and smiling, she pushed herself up and walked into the kitchen.

Opening the phone as I got to my knees and then stood up, I said, still panting, "Hey, Dani, I was just going to call you...right after I got done beating up my old man."

She laughed on the other end and said, "He need a good butt whoopin' again?"

"Yep, hard to believe, I know." I giggled into the phone.

Her voice calmed, and concern filled the phone, "Seriously, Sami, Mandy called me last night. You okay? How's Mark?"

Moving toward the door, I answered, "I'm okay. Mom and Dad are hanging in there, and Mark looks like he made out with an explosive device." Not wanting to wreck the mood in the room, I went back out into the hall to continue our conversation.

As I was leaving the room, she asked, "Is he going to be okay?"

The door bumped shut behind me, and I felt safe to answer her question. Talking softly so as to not annoy Nurse Ratchet, I filled her in on everything that had happened from the minute I opened my locker at school yesterday to right now. Stunned and disappointed, she asked, "Why didn't you call me?"

"Sorry, Dan, everything happened so fast." I paused and took a deep breath. "I'm scared," I admitted. "…and…and I didn't want you to worry. You're not supposed to have any stress if you're going to get better."

She jumped in, "Hey, I'm great. Don't worry about me. I only have one more treatment. Then no more nasty farts for me." We both laughed as we reminisced for a few minutes about all the times we'd been together, enjoying the wonderful aromas chemotherapy had created.

Pulling the subject back to where we started, Dani said softly, "Sam, Mark's in good hands, and he's tough. He'll be okay."

"Dr. K said it's a miracle he's still alive." I choked on my words as they came out.

Dani heard it in my voice, and without flinching demanded, "Hey, meet me in the front lobby of the hospital at five."

Surprised and confused, I asked, "You're coming here?"

"Yeah," she answered. "As soon as I hung up with Mandy last night, I had Mom change my chemo appointment to Mayo for the afternoon. You can come with, and we can hang out."

"Seriously, you can do that?" I asked, astounded.

"Sure. Now get back and give your dad some more crap from me," she joked.

"Deal," I said and hung up the phone. I was so happy she was coming that not even the evil death stares of the nurse in charge could stop me from happily skipping back to our room. Positive thoughts gushed though my entire soul, and I was gushing in amazement at her strength and energy. I hoped even just a bit would rub off on Mark. If he could get some of that, I knew he'd be fine.

My hope and strength renewed after talking to the one person in the world I respect the most, I bounded back to our family room once again. This time my parents weren't making out on the couch; they were gone. Scared, I left the room, quickly scrubbed up with the hand sanitizer, and hesitantly entered the ICU. From just beyond the doors, I could see the side of my mom's head through a window in Mark's room. I didn't know what to feel. This was the first time they'd gone in without telling me, and I wasn't sure what the haste of their visit meant. My pace quickened as I approached the doorway of my big brother's room. As I passed through the ICU nurse's station just outside his door, I could see him perfectly. He was sitting up in bed, talking lazily to my parents. When I entered the room, he shifted his eyes to meet mine and said, "Hey, Saaaa." Then he shot me a totally lopsided smile.

Mom looked at me and explained, "Mark only has use of his left side right now, sweetie, but that will most likely heal in time."

Mark interjected, "Goo thig I lef anded." We all laughed.

"It obviously didn't affect his sense of humor," Dr. Kumada said.

I didn't ask, but Mom saw the confused look on my face every time he spoke. Nodding to Dr. Kumada then turning to look at me, Mom reassuringly said, "Don't worry about how he pronounces things now. His speech is labored but will come back with time and therapy."

Trying to be serious, I said, "Come on, don't fix that. I like the way he talks, especially when it makes him drool on himself."

Mark instinctively reached for his chin with his left hand. When he touched his totally dry chin, he scowled at me as best he could and tried to give me the finger. Even Dr. Kumada burst out laughing.

"Okay, family, nap time," Dr. Kumada said as our laughter started to fade away. "We don't want to get him too stirred up yet. There'll be plenty of time for that later." She smiled. We all got the drift and said our good-byes to Mark. When I went to give him a kiss on the cheek, he said something so inaudible that the only thing we could make out was that he called me "little poo." We all burst out laughing again, and, instead of kissing his cheek, I gently bit it. He clubbed me as best he could with his left arm.

Stepping away from his bed and toward the door, I looked back. Right then, I knew in my heart that he was going to be just fine. Before I was totally out of the room, I said, "See ya later, alligator." He smiled, waved clumsily, and started to nod off to sleep from the medicine Dr. K had given him a few minutes ago. Once we were all in the hall, settled in on a conversation with Dr. Kumada and her nurse about what was going to happen next, I peeked into one of Mark's windows, and he was already fast asleep.

After talking to Dr. K, my parents and I went to the cafeteria for brunch, and I filled them in on my conversations with DJ and Danielle. They were excited that my friends were all coming. I think maybe they were more excited to get me out of their hair for a while so they could smooch in private without me interrupting every five minutes.

Mom took a bite of her cheeseburger and said, "I love that they're coming. We should go to the gift shop and get some games for you and Dani to play while she's having her treatment."

Thankful but annoyed, I said, "Mom, we're a little too old for games." I stuffed a handful of French fries into my mouth and said, "Besides, we have so much to talk about, there won't be time for games."

Giving me her best disgusted look, Mom scolded me, "Honey, ladies don't talk with their mouths full."

I swallowed, sighed, and apologized, "Sorry, Mom, but right now, given what has taken place in the past few days, manners totally aren't at the top of my list of things to do."

As I wiped my hands on the napkin in my lap, Mom reached over and placed her hand on top of mine. "Sam, everything's going to be fine."

Then Dad started the conversation we've all been dreading. "Okay girls, what are we going to tell Detective Renner when he comes?"

Surprised at his question, I asked, "What do you mean 'what are we going to tell him?' That's pretty obvious isn't it? Monte's the spawn of Satan and should be put away forever, or better yet, burned at the stake!" After the words left my lips, a dead silence fell across the dining room. When I looked around, everyone was staring at me. I hadn't even realized that I'd yelled my last sentence. Lowering my gaze to my lap, a tear fell onto my napkin, and I whispered, "I'm sorry. That was harsh."

Ignoring the stares, Dad reached over and rubbed the back of my head. Gently he asked, "Sam, you're right. He's an animal, and the police will make sure he pays for what he's done." He paused. "I guess what I was really asking is ..."—he paused longer this time—"is that, now that you're seventeen, you'll be talking to the detective without us. Are you ready for that? Would you like to talk to us about it first?" I shook my head no. He went on. "Honey, he's done some horrible things, and given the fact that you spent so much time with him when you were little at Grandma and Grandpa's house, we're worried that he may have hurt you some way too."

Panic swept my entire body. My self-preservation instinct kicked in, and I dramatically shoved my tray to the center of the table, got up, and ran for the door. It was like I wasn't in control of my body. I couldn't stop myself from running. When I got outside, I stopped in a grassy area around the corner of the building. A wave of nausea came over me, and my legs went numb. I dropped to all fours and wretched furiously in the grass. Then next thing I remember is the feeling of floating I got every time I passed out in school and someone picked me up to take me to the nurse's office.

From somewhere outside my head, I heard a voice. "Sam, honey?" The bouncing continued. "Open your eyes, sweetie. It's Daddy." I heard an electric door slide open and a gush of wind hit my face.

"Daddy's here. It's okay." I could hear my dad talking and tried to respond, but for some reason, I couldn't make my eyes open. The next thing I knew, I felt something cold and hard under my back and heard people rushing around me.

"Ow," I whispered, barely audible as a sharp poke stuck my arm, and a cold stinging sensation seeped upward.

"Samantha, open your eyes," a strange, low voice commanded gently from directly above my face.

Peeling my eyes open, I said, "Who are you?" I reached up to rub my eyes, but the motion was halted by a tugging feeling. Remembering the shackles that bound my arms and legs in my dream, I screamed, "Where am I? Daddy!"

Pressing firmly on my arms to keep me from hurting myself, the low voice spoke to me comfortingly. "Whoa, honey, relax. Lay still. You have an IV in your hand to get some fluids into you quickly. We can take it out as soon as this bag is empty."

Peeking through the slits I was able to create in my eyes, I relaxed and mumbled, "Whoa yourself." I paused and rubbed my eyes. "Am I in heaven 'cause I've never seen a boy as pretty as you on earth," I said through the fog in my brain.

Sounding a little embarrassed, Dad said, "Sorry, you'll have to excuse her. Every time she's coming out of one of her fainting episodes, her verbal filter takes longer to come back than she does." I could hear both of them get a good chuckle at my expense. Nice thing was, when I was in this particular state of mind, I didn't care.

"No problem," the beautiful male nurse said. Then he reached up and gave the fluids bag a big squeeze. "Let's get this process moving, shall we?"

Instantly, I felt the sensation that I had to pee, and my filter leaked once again. "I need to shake the dew off my lily. Could you please take that thing out of my arm, or I'm going to pee right on your pretty little white outfit."

He and my dad laughed again, and I felt tape being pulled off my arm. "Sure thing, little lady. I can tell by your newly restored attitude that you're going to be just fine."

Dad couldn't help contributing to my harassment. "He's got your number, Sami."

The beautiful man lifted my head, helping me to a sitting position, "Stay there for a second."

"A second is all I've got, pretty boy," I smarted off, causing my mom to choke back a giggle from somewhere behind me.

"Okay, let's get you to the bathroom," he said, trying to sound professional, but I could hear the giggle in his voice. Truthfully, I was totally awake, but it was kind of fun having this beautiful man draped all over me. I thought I'd suck it up just a couple more seconds.

Dad caught on and said, "Okay, Sam, pee and let's get back upstairs."

I laughed, and then not only my dad knew I was playing, but the nurse knew as well. He playfully punched me in the shoulder and said, "You big faker. You got me." We all laughed as I shut the door to the ladies' room. I could hear the two of them and my mom outside joking about my "filter" as I took care of business.

When I relaxed, the cause of my syncope came flooding back, and my pulse quickened. My mind spun through the decisions I was going to have to make soon. What was I going to tell the detective? *Should I tell him everything that happened or just about the stuff he already knew. I hope DJ, Mandy, and Dani get here before he does. It would really help to talk to them first.*

Finishing up with my business in the bathroom, I rejoined my parents, only to discover the nurse had gone back to his duties. Dad put his arm around my shoulder and said, "Let's go back upstairs and lie down for awhile. A good nap will do us all good."

I couldn't help but notice that he avoided the subject of what caused this episode to begin with. As we passed the gift shop, Mom grabbed my arm and asked, "Feel like checking it out?" Giving me her best puppy dog look, she added, "Looks like they have some pretty cute stuff in there." Then, not giving me time to decide, she grabbed my hand and pulled me into the store. She loved to shop, and it made me want to vomit. Oh well, I probably owed her one since I pulled that stunt at lunch.

As we entered the store, I looked around and saw that they really did have pretty stuff. I made my way to the back and found shelves and shelves of the most awesome flip flops on the planet. There were dozens of colors all loaded down with bling. "Mom, check these out!" I yelled across the store.

Mom came over and, breathing heavily in excitement, gasped, "Wow, how much?"

"I don't know. I was afraid to look." Picking up a pair of black with multicolored beads, I carefully flipped over the price tag. Not able to hide my surprise, I blurted loudly, "Twelve ninety-nine. Holy crap, let's get some!"

Embarrassed, Mom shot me a look that held angry eyes and a smile, "Sam, your mouth."

Not the least bit embarrassed, I whispered loudly, "Sorry, Mom. Can we?"

Her face relaxed into a big smile, and she said, "Sure, pick out a couple pair." Turning over a pair in her own hands and inspecting them thoroughly she sighed. "These are too cute to pass up."

For once, I was actually having fun shopping. As I shuffled through all the different shoes trying them on and shuffling some more, I finally decided on a pair of black ones with the brightly colored beads and white ones with rhinestones. Happy with my selection, I hooked the elastic holding the two sandals together around my finger and, swinging them proudly, found my mom over by the books.

"Nice purchase, Sami girl." She smiled, checking out the sandals I dangled in her face proudly.

Through a sly smile, I planted a seed. "Now all we need is for Mark to get better so we can go on vacation somewhere super warm."

She nudged me with her whole body as she passed me in the aisle and agreed, "You know, when this is all over, a vacation sounds like a great idea."

Mom picked out a new book and a couple of magazines, I got my flip flops, and Dad, of course, found some of the grossest candy. We made our purchases and headed up to the family room. In the elevator, Dad looked at his watch and said, "Wow, we've been gone a long time. It's already four. I bet your friends and Detective Renner will be here soon if they aren't already."

Mom looked at me, obviously afraid of my reaction to the mention of Detective Renner's name. I sighed. "Don't worry. I'm okay, Mom."

The familiar ding of the elevator bounced off the walls of our metal transport, and as we stepped out onto our floor, a matching door opened across the hall, and out stepped all of our company. Relief flushed my every capillary at the sight of my beloved friends. Instinctively, I fell into their arms in a three-way hug as my parents shook hands with the detective. We fell instantly in to natural conversation as we walked to our room. It was going to be an interesting evening.

Mom, Dad, and Detective Renner went into the room, and DJ, Mandy, and I went to the end of the hall where I liked to hang out in the big squishy chairs and watch the traffic below as I talked on the phone. When we were all settled in, I said, "Dani is coming to Mayo for her chemo at five. It'll be nice to all hang out without adults for a while."

"Don't the nurses have to be in there?" Mandy asked.

"Yeah, but they don't count. They're sworn to secrecy," I answered.

"Good ol' HIPAA," DJ added. "Hey, Sam, that detective seems like a good guy."

Mandy interjected, "Huge guy."

"We got to talk to him a bit in the elevator," DJ said, ignoring her comment.

She giggled, "He barely fit in there. Should be Detective Ogre, not Detective Renner."

Dizzy from the two of them, I finally said, "Hey, my brain is fried. How 'bout we have one conversation at a time." Realizing they'd both had been talking at the same time about different things, they looked at each other and started laughing.

Too embarrassed to tell them what had happened at lunch, I avoided the subject altogether and went right past the detective comments. "So, how's school…anything weird going on there?"

I could see Mandy started to squirm in her seat, practically coming out of her skin. It was like my asking that question was her cue to open the floodgates. "Oh my gosh, Sam, the rumors are flying like a swarm of killer bees. Becky and her flock have totally mellowed out. They've even been asking about Mark's condition and if you're okay or not. It's pretty strange." Without ever stopping to take a breath, Mandy kept on full steam ahead. "Oh yeah, and in town, people are scared because they're keeping freak boy right in the city jail. The cops have had to break up packs of angry men carrying shotguns outside the jail." Her description of the chaos at home went on for several minutes.

When she finally stopped to take a breath, DJ seized the moment to get a word in, "Sam, you have to tell Detective Renner everything. If you don't, he might get out."

Subdued, I looked at the floor and said, "I know."

Shifting in his chair to close the gap between us, he said more quietly this time, "Seriously, you can't leave anything out." He touched my hand, "…not anything…no matter what."

"I know," I repeated, quietly tucking my legs up to my chest and wrapping my arms around my knees. It was a position I knew well in my seventeen years, one of safety.

My friends and I talked for hours. Dani got there at around four thirty, and we all trudged down to the chemo lab to continue our conversation. It was so great to see her again. She was awfully thin, but who wouldn't be after what she'd been through? Other than being skinny, we all thought she looked great. It was so nice having normal kid conversation. I hadn't realized how much I'd missed that lately. Suddenly, there was a knock on the door. Mom peeked her head in and said softly, "Sami, it's your turn to talk to Detective Renner."

Without hesitation, Dani shouted, "Send him in!"

I looked at her shocked, "Can he come in here?"

"Sure, I'm the boss in here, and I say bring it on," she said with mock authority.

Mom shrugged her shoulders and said, "Okay. I wouldn't want to cheese off the boss."

"Oh my gosh, your mom must be stressed out. That's when she makes up the best sayings." Dani giggled.

"No kidding." I smirked. "She's been so quiet lately. I worry about her," I said, instantly serious.

Just then, there was another knock on the door, and Dani yelled, "Come in Detective Og—I mean, Renner." We all snickered, and I reached over and smacked her on the knee.

Detective Renner poured his oversized frame through the normal-sized doorway and looked like Shrek. We all noticed his awkwardness and giggled under our breath. Noticing our amusement, he said, "I know. I never fit anywhere. Being six-foot-seven inches has its advantages and disadvantages."

Feeling bad for the big man, I said, "Detective, everyone at school always teases that size doesn't matter. Now I know what they're talking about. It's okay to be big."

Whatever I just said must have had a totally different connotation than the sincerity I actually meant by it, because everyone in the room, even the nurses, just about peed themselves in laughter. Even Detective Renner blew spit all over the place as he doubled over.

"What?" I said, confused. "Really, big isn't bad, just like small isn't bad." This actually made it worse, and even the doctor on the other side of the room couldn't hold it in any longer. "Okay, you jerks, laugh if you want." I tried to be mad, but laughter was contagious, and I couldn't restrain myself anymore. I let it fly and laughed until I cried.

Once we all had ourselves pulled back together again, Detective Renner started the questioning. Getting started was difficult, but with the help and prodding of my friends, I told him things that even they didn't know about. I spilled everything and didn't stop until I was so mentally and emotionally exhausted that I felt the way a dishrag must feel after it's been rung out to the very last drop. In fact, that's exactly how my muscles felt. When I was finished talking, I leaned back in my chair, let my head fall into the soft abyss of the cushion, and shut my eyes. For the billionth time in the past few days, they burned from the threat of tears. I didn't want to cry, but I didn't have any energy left to hold it in. As the detective got a few more details from my friends, I sat quietly in my chair, legs pulled up tight against my chest with my arms wrapped around my knees. Without saying a word, silently, warm streams fell from the corners of both eyes. It was over. My secret had been revealed, and there was no going back. I couldn't help but wonder how my life would change.

CHAPTER TWENTY-SEVEN

When DJ and Amanda went back to home, my parents convinced me it was best if I went with them. As DJ drove, I sat in the backseat, invisible and quiet, contemplating how life would forever be different. I didn't want to leave Mom, Dad, and Mark, but I knew if I stayed, I would never catch up with my schoolwork.

Mom called Mandy's mom, and they arranged for me to stay at their house during the week. DJ offered to bring me to Mayo on the weekends, and my parents insisted on paying him for his gas, time, and the use of his car.

As I thought of what the next few months were going to be like, I was consumed by stress. Not only was Mark going to have a long, treacherous recovery, but everyone at home and around the entire area now knew my secret. We all had Monte LaReaux to thank for all our hell on earth. *Monte, what is to become of Monte?* I thought.

Trying not to scare me, Mandy turned in her seat to look at me and said, "Only ten more miles, Sam. How ya doin'?" She tried to smile, and I forced one in return.

"'Kay," Was all I could muster the energy to say.

In the rearview mirror, I saw DJ's eyes shift to look directly into mine. He quietly said, "It'll be fine. You have us."

Forcing another smile, I sighed, "Thanks, guys. What would I do without you?" I paused just long enough for my words to hit my eardrums and then I spat, "Wait, I don't even want to know what I'd do without you. You can't ever leave me." Mandy reached her arm back, and I grabbed her hand in mine. Nothing needed to be said.

Several minutes later, DJ shouted cheerfully from the driver's seat, "Honey, we're home."

Unsnapping my seatbelt, I scooted up to the edge of my seat to get a better view out of the front window. "Looks quiet," I said.

"Quiet is good," Mandy added. "D, wanna come over for awhile?" she asked.

"Sure. What's for dinner?" He chuckled, keeping his eyes on the road.

From the backseat I teased, "Who cares? You'd eat liver and on-ions if someone made it for you."

Shaking his head in agreement he said, "Good point. Sure."

As we pulled into Mandy's driveway, her parents came out to greet us. I couldn't help but look over my shoulder. Being here made me nervous, even if the cops had Monte in the jail. Just knowing he was in this town scared me.

After a nice dinner of no liver and onions, DJ, Mandy, and I went over to my house to get clothes for the next few days. It felt good to be home, but when I walked past Mark's room, it felt like an elephant was sitting on my chest. I couldn't breathe. My legs buckled a little, and DJ wrapped his arm around my waist. It's okay, little one. He'll be home soon."

Not able to hold back tears, I mumbled, "I know. It's just still fresh."

From behind me Mandy said, "Time will not only heal him, but you too."

As we entered my room, I went straight to my closet and pulled out my duffel bag. Tossing it onto the floor, I asked, "Mandy, wanna grab me some undies and socks? D, can you grab the hair dryer and curling iron from the bathroom?"

"Sure," she said, standing to help.

From his perch on my bed, DJ tried to sound offended, "Why can't I get your undies and she get your hair junk?

Laughing at him, I smarted off, "'Cause she'll just put them in my bag and not run around with them on her head. Duh!"

As I turned back to the clothes in the closet, I was struck from behind by one of the stuffed animals on my bed. Trying to act pissed, I reached down, grabbed the bear, and chucked it back at DJ... shooting far to the right, of course. He fell back onto my bed, laughing hysterically. "You throw like a girl!"

"I am a girl, you dork." I sneered. "And don't you forget it."

The banter continued the entire time we packed. I think both of my friends were trying to keep my mind off what was really going on.

When I had everything I needed to get me through the week, DJ dropped Mandy and I off at her house and went home.

"See you two at school tomorrow!" He shouted out his car window as he backed out of the driveway.

"If you're lucky!" I yelled back.

Mandy grabbed my hand and pulled me toward her front door. I watched DJ's car until it was no longer visible.

"Stay safe," I muttered under my breath and then followed her into the safety of her house.

CHAPTER TWENTY-EIGHT

The rest of my year came and went. I was so busy with homework, practice, meets, and running back and forth to the Mayo to see Mark and my parents that I couldn't even tell if the girls were nasty or not. Frankly, I didn't care. I just did my thing and lived as much as I could. For the first time since I can remember, I felt free and safe. Monte had been found guilty of numerous felonies…murder, arson, stalking, molestation; thankfully, the list was endless. Once he turns twenty-one, they're going to move him to the penitentiary where he will spend the rest of his natural-born life.

That summer, I went back to the cities, but club wasn't my only destination. Not only was I close enough to Mark to go back and forth every day, but the coach from the university was actively recruiting me and wanted me to spend time working out with him and the girls on the team.

One day when I was at the gym, Coach came over and told me I had a phone call.

"Who is it?" I asked, confused as I followed him back to his office.

"I think it's your mom," he said as we entered the little room.

Handing me the phone, he said, "Here you go."

I hesitated to take it from him. "You're due for some good news," he assured me.

"Thanks," I said and took the receiver. Slowly, I lifted it to my ear and said, "Hello?"

"Honey, we're going home!" my mom's excited voice shouted from the other end of the line.

"What?" I asked, not sure I understood what she meant.

"Mark! He's going home!" she shouted again, her excitement bubbling over into the phone.

I couldn't move. Shock had taken over my body, "When?" I asked.

"Tomorrow. Can you come down?" she said, trying to hide the fact that she was crying.

"I'm leaving right now!" I spat into the phone. "See you in an hour."

"Okay, drive safe," Mom said and hung up.

I couldn't stop the tears as I bounced up to my coach. "He's coming home!" I shouted as I threw my arms around him and jumped in a circle, dragging him along with me.

Coach freed himself from my death grip, and, as I stepped away still giggling and crying and bouncing, slapped me on the butt and said, "What are you waiting for, get out of here already!" That's all he had to say. As I ran out of the gym, I hastily hugged everyone I saw, even the janitor.

I didn't think I'd ever get to Mayo, but when I did, I was too excited to wait for the elevator, so I bounded up the stairs two at a time. When I bashed through the door to his floor, I nearly knocked Mom off her feet. "Samantha, my goodness. Slow down. You nearly killed me," she scolded.

Nothing could bring me down. I scooped her up in my arms and bounced around in circle. As I turned, I saw a familiar face out of the corner of my tear-filled eye, and I stopped in my tracks. "Mark!" I screamed. "You're walking!" I left my mom and ran over to my brother, hugging him gently for a long, long time. When I finally released him, he said. "Les go home, Mousey Girl."